THE
COMPASS
STONE

THE COMPASS STONE

Fernando Arrabal

TRANSLATED BY
Andrew Hurley

GROVE PRESS *New York*

Published by Grove Press, Inc.
920 Broadway
New York, N.Y. 10010

Library of Congress Cataloging-in-Publication Data

Arrabal, Fernando.
    The compass stone.

    Originally published as: La piedra iluminada.
    I. Title.
PQ6601.R58P5413   1987   863'.64   87-12120
ISBN 0-8021-0002-3

Designed by Irving Perkins Associates
Manufactured in the United States of America
First Edition 1987

10 9 8 7 6 5 4 3 2 1

Translator's Note

THE COPYIST DID HIS WORK OF BRING-
ing the infant *memoir* to the light, and then I was entrusted with my own stranger task of transporting the creature
over a sea of perilous crossing. I have been accompanied
and aided by three ladies who many times saved me from
fatal shipboard slips. They are María Soledad Rodríguez,
Ada Marie Vilar de Kerkhoff, and Isabel Garayta. The new-
naturalized thing is indebted for its ultramarine existence to
those ever watchful governesses; any bruises on its counte-
nance, or misshapen limbs, are due solely to my own clumsy
care, and are none of their own. On the voyage I had the
benefit of a strange book's company, *La Reverdie,* the same
father's child, a twin I believe of the babe I had been entrusted
with, and a useful as well as good companion. Had it not been
for these aids and accomplices, this servant's task would un-
doubtedly have miscarried. My deep thanks go to them.

THE
COMPASS
STONE

Copyist's Note

IN A PLACE CALLED—BUT I WOULD PRE-
fer not to remember its name—, half a world distant from
the place of my birth, I came across a packet of manuscript
pages tied up in saffron-coloured ribbon. Great was my surprise to find in those latitudes, which I had taken to be far gone
in age and decrepitude, a *memoir* couched in my native tongue.

I exhumed the bundle from a heap of crumpled, withered
papers piled into the corner of a large hall, the heart of an
ill-restored ruin which at its high-water mark had been a palace
and at its ebb an inn for vagrants.

Again and again I pored through the manuscript. On a
second reading I made easier way; it seemed less complex and
yet even more fantastic than at first. I had racked my brains
many times over the convolutions of the memoirist's script
during my first hours of reading, and even oftener the indecipherable hand had produced in me anxious moments of suspense and anticipation, until at last I found I could let myself
be carried along on its lines like a kite snatched up by the wind
after several fitful but fruitless starts.

On the following day, on the lee side of a third reading, it
occurred to me to draw a plan of the Mansion, using only the
light thrown on it by the young woman's description. I reproduce it here in that same spirit of spontaneity: but although it
is true that this sketch is congruent in broad outline with the
description set down by the chronicler, and with the general
aspect of the building, it is no less true that in its angularity

the plan loses many of the sinuosities and still more of the
fire-lit twists and turns of the edifice, while still scrupulously
reproducing, as I say, the essence of its geometry.

PLAN OF THE MANSION

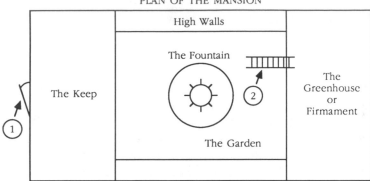

(1) Sole door opening to the outside
(2) Ladder for ascending into the Greenhouse

None of the facts I have since collected merits mention, nor
do those I have picked up which bear on the crimes, nor those
I have gathered concerning the memoirist's father ("the
Maimed One") and the two women outside the family
("the Sisters") who shared his life in the Keep. There is little
I might add to what the authoress reveals to us about the
wrestler K— and the aesthete (and apprentice detective) S—.
As for the illustrious painters P— and D—, it is obvious that
there is much that I might say, and even more that I should
not.

A friend of mine, an aged dame, a saintly woman as ana-
chronistic as she is touching, begged me to suppress certain
"frightful" passages or, at the least, mercifully, to preface the
book with this dedication:

> In memory of those men who, believing
> they had just reached the gates of Glory,
> fell headlong, throats slashed, into
> the Pit.

Thus, dear reader, this account, in which in so singular a fashion meditation, ardour, and spiritual quest come together, is not my own. I must then add nothing to the manuscript nor in any way seek to soften or improve it with my own emendations: just as I discovered it, I send it to press, even knowing that its interrogative style may seem somewhat forced or stilted, its semantics startling, and not a few of its revelations disconcerting or, at the very least, most uncommon among our letters. These were, I must admit, my initial misgivings as well.

And yet, let us allow the protagonist's story to speak for itself.

The STRANGER BLINDLY CLUTCHED AT me from where he lay between the seats of the Cinema. His senses were in a swoon, all caution had deserted him. I sought to have my pleasure of him without arousing his attention; his senses drugged, I might draw the blade across his throat. Hours earlier, in the Firmament, I had readied myself for the Soirée; I had dropped the razor in my purse.

The greenhouse, where I dwelt, a domain of Natural Law, was called the Firmament. I was the only person who lived within its realm. To the West, like some machine upraised in threat, stood a tyranny—the Keep. It housed but three sole inhabitants, the Sisters and the Maimed One. The Garden was the sea that separated these two continents, and yet the two refuges coexisted, by virtue of the rude high walls which, like great arms, pulled the two dwellings into one geographical unity, one globe, a space known as the Mansion. The alliance of the Firmament and the Keep was fixed by treaties, never written, however, nor even alluded to. In exchange for my silence, the Maimed One provided aid toward the maintenance of the Firmament. I, like the trinity of monkeys, was to all intents blind, deaf, and mute—I saw, heard, spoke nothing of what passed in the Keep. Peace was the constant byword of our relations, although from time to time there would be clumsy overtures, probes from the Maimed One, aimed at consummating a closer association; his sieges, beseeching, would seek to shake the cold walls of insensibility that stood between us:

"You are eighteen years old, and you are my daughter. Why will you not come live with us in the Keep? For years you have cloistered yourself there, back behind the Garden, in that huge wild wreck the greenhouse has fallen into."

A powerful current of fatalism shaped life within the Keep, replacing the triumphalism which years ago had graced it. That current of pessimism lent an air of hopes gone adrift and sour to its three inhabitants, as though a silence were rising, swelling in their souls, a tide of sure oblivion washing over them. The death of the gardener and the dismissal of the last two servants accentuated the Maimed One's dejection:

"I have suffered so. . . . You cannot imagine how life, the world, . . . you . . . have disappointed me. When I see you climb that ladder and crawl in that broken window in the greenhouse . . . my despair overwhelms me! What have I done to you, why do you treat me so?"

Shielded by thick walls and parapets, at the foot of the Vigorous Mountains, loomed the Castle of Merits. It commanded the Northern Firmament. Its fortifications stood stiff, erect, and forbidding, parings of my fingernails bristling in the embrasures of the loopholes. With a long straw wand I managed to introduce into the Throne Room the postman's button, the piece of necktie I severed in the Cinema, and a match from the porter at the Conservatory.

It was just striking ten o'clock at night when I went into the Cinema with the stranger. The words P— had exclaimed to me, three years before, when he gave me the cameo and the razor, suddenly came to my mind:

"To think about eternity, or the possibility of never dying, at my age! It is horrifying! . . . Today I am exactly ninety-one years and five months old, to the day. I would never show a single grey hair, or a wrinkle, or a day more or less. . . . If I were fifteen, like you . . ."

The screen in the Cinema stood just at the entrance. The theatre was almost deserted at that hour. Row 20, at the rear, stood at the border of no-man's-land—a belly of shadow gored by the horns of destiny. The stranger took me to the last row.

How was one to interpret the legends and beliefs that had grown up in the greenhouse to explain the creation of the Firmament? Most of them exalted its origins, lending them a paradisal cast. These legends declared that once upon a time the ground and the glass panes above it were connected, undivided, until one day the sky was separated from the land. The Firmament then became the hub and centre of the universe. Its capital was built where all its lines converged and was comprised of a *suite* of structures I erected with slivers and withes and odd pieces of wood. In the Plaza of the Preceptress was set the Calendar—a clay disc marked with graduated points, rays, and symbols of varying size. In the Plaza of the East the dwarf cedar which K— had given me displayed its changing colours throughout the cycle of the year. When it seemed that one colour was about to fade away, the next one was born, what had begun in pallor and lividness springing forth in a blaze of hues and pigments. Every thing that existed belonged to its own well-defined category in the Firmament. As a consequence, each category partook of the attributes and virtues inherent in the realities which it contained. And yet, thanks to a daring system of correspondences, each category also demonstrated the affinities that obtained between all the elements of the greenhouse. For example, even cockroaches, ticks, ants, flies, were integrated into the scheme of the Firmament. They comprised an analogy among themselves and, at the same time, were, together, the symbol of complementarity and of variety, choice. When a unicorn caterpillar slept, that symbolized the time of darkness, decrepitude and absence, placidity, suspension; when it awoke, the time of light, strength and plenitude, zeal, activity. Taken not separately but together, they made the cycle Day–Night, formed by the coming together of two opposite yet linked and complementary states, balanced extremes which, inextricably intertwined, declared Harmony.

Before he took me to the Cinema, the stranger approached me. Was he fearful? Nervous? Irresolute? Was he sixty years old? Fifty? He introduced himself. We went first to a bar. He repeated again and again that he owned a great deal of land. In my bag I was carrying the gift that P— had given me.

The greenhouse, before my birth, had been guarded by a mastiff. One night a raptor came down from the sky and ripped the dog's throat open with one great slash of its beak. Was that the first day of creation? If so, did the Firmament come into being, then, as the result of a sacrifice? Did the mastiff's decomposing flesh create the land?, his bones, the Crags of Dogma?, his blood, the waters of the Vat?, his fur, the plants?, his skull, the glass panes of the roof? To ensure the regeneration of life in the Firmament, and its cohesion, did that sacrifice have to be repeated, renewed? Painful immolations fueled by poisoned cream be conceived? Were the stars outside these walls born from the sparks of pain flashing from the mastiff in his last moments of agony?

The stranger took me to the last row of the theatre. There was an odour of resin mixed with some indefinite perfume.

Candle-fly behaviour had not altered since I had taken up residence in the greenhouse. With no prior experience novices performed the rites of procreation. From the first act of the ceremony, they went unerringly through the complex stages which led them to copulation. Did this constitute unlearned behaviour? Did the Firmament impress the candle-fly with the lesson at the moment it blew life into the fly? With his left wing held to his abdomen, the male would zigzag along behind the female, rapidly fluttering his outspread right wing. Was the melody thereby produced a nuptial hymn? A *nocturne* fallen to earth from dreams? A buzzing laden with menace? Were candle-flies born with all the movements already learned? Did the dance translate them to a plane of consciousness prior to their existence? Had each movement been laid down since the moment of the Firmament's creation? When they came to the ritual's conclusion, the abdomen above executed a complicated contortion to penetrate the abdomen beneath. What was the purpose, end, of so much energy?, so much dynamism?, so much repetition in seeming spontaneity? Was the cruel siege crowned by this final battering? Did the abrupt *coup de grace* consummate the attack? And after that unbearable extreme of tension, after that eruption, did candle-flies achieve the sense of having been large-expanded in littleness? Still isolated terms in the void?

Why did I have the impression that slimy hands were emerging from the thorax of the stranger? Between them I still watched the film. Aeroplanes were flying in pursuit of one another. A harsh drone filled the theatre.

After the creation of the Firmament I built temples, museums, theatres, sanctuaries, palaces, and monasteries from cigar boxes; I traced out roads with sand; I drilled wells with pencils and made up a water-wheel out of thimbles. Porcelain plates formed the beds of lakes, and the vault of heaven was all that could be seen through the great glass panes of the greenhouse. Such places as the Institute of the Species or the Chamber of Destiny were rumoured, but there was no proof of their actual existence. The greenhouse, as the navel of the universe, was the point where the sky outside and the subterranean regions beneath the Empire of the Ants were connected. Every theory which attempted to explain how the Firmament was created referred to the first moments of its existence as the time when divisions could add nothing to its primordial splendour, as the marvellous epoch of the First Time.

In the Cinema the pilots were fighting—warriors, heroes, traitors. The aeroplanes roared, their machine guns stuttered. The stranger's fingers dug into me. How many fingers? I could hear the growling, grunting sounds he uttered. Was he groaning? Purring? Was he seeking to reach perfect knowledge? To attain a state of catalepsy? To taste the joys of beatitude? What secret of life was he longing to penetrate with his fingers? Did he burn to hold and touch the heart of the universe? To feel its throbbing? Would he stop at an exploration of external form or did he hope to find happiness to surpass that of the most fortunate viceroy butterfly? The heroism of the film's leading man, the thick grainy sweat oozing down his bronze skin—did that inspire the stranger to forge onward?

In the greenhouse there stood an infinite oak tree which no
one could see. Its highest leaves touched the sky, its branches
embraced all the Firmament, and its roots were buried in the
Country of the Dead. The dwarf cedar, K—'s *bonsai,* was but
its microcosmic symbol. It was thought that the Firmament
would come to an end the day a swarm of bayonet-beetles
devoured the leaves of the invisible tree, the lizards rotted its
trunk with rivers of urine, and the soldier-ants gnawed away
its roots. Was all this a paradox? And this paradox, did it in
turn, fecund, overspread all things? Did it manifest the inde-
structible unity of the essence of the Firmament? Did it dictate
caution in gainsaying, in attack, in antagonism, and counsel
circumspection even in the throes of ecstasy?

The stranger knelt between the legs-of-my-body. He covered my thighs with babbled drool and spit. In that position
his hands and arms did not block my view of the screen. The
aeroplanes had stopped their circling and spinning and diving.
With his forehead pressed to my navel, he emitted undefinable
sounds. Was he praying? Sobbing? Softly neighing? All the
foulest-smelling, dirtiest, most vile weight my body was bur-
dened with was where his interest lay. Did those zones ooze
and drip with spirituality? For him?, or in general? His sound
grew, the rhythm changed. Was it a whispered song? A murmur from his soul? A snort from his instincts? What was it the
stranger sought within me? Was he deep-sea diving? Was he
trying to pass through fire without being burned? Why was he
feeling his way with such constant urgency? Did he believe
that place he sought to reach would render him immortal?
Intelligent? Happy? What was he discovering inside me?
He climbed hills, crossed frontiers, cleared away obstacles,
forded valleys, explored clefts and gullies, caverns, nauseat-
ing grottoes. Did he plunge into that foetidness to tap the
fountain-source of energy? Of spontaneity? Of life itself?

On the screen, tanks vomited forth bursts of fire at the
aeroplanes. Sparks flared. The warriors' faces were black with
soot and ash, like primitive shamans.

In the Firmament, the stars shone like lighted rooms suspended from the sky, outside the walls. They had never known the chaos which had existed in the greenhouse before my coming there. That is why they shone throughout the night and disappeared during the day. What part did those celestial materials play—did they contribute the element requisite to the Firmament's spirituality? That exquisitely strait place in which I myself breathed—was it a preserve of harmony?

The stranger stretched lengthwise on the floor between the seats of the theatre.

"Come."

His voice was muffled. His hands twined around the legs-of-my-body. Tentacles like choppy waves. Were they emerging from this mass of fat? They scrabbled at my feet. Were they seeking the dark? The intimate? The aeroplanes took off again, landed. They flew into the sky, or they descended, sheathed in flames, to the centre of the earth.

"Come."

The most-repugnant-part-of-my-body—did it truly contain such inspiration? So much knowledge? So much light? Could the stranger have perceived, as he fondled and groped about me, that one mystery would be added to another? Did he think that all of them plaited and wound together would form the Gate of Wonders? Did his will grow faint?, his reason sicken?, his acuteness become dull? Once he was sated and exhausted, would his discretion lapse into indiscretion?

The banded butterflies of the Firmament—would they have chosen to be born from an egg's tears?, or for the Firmament itself to be the flower sprouted from the phlegm spat out by a grasshopper of light? For the window-panes and the Vat, the deserts and the volcanoes, the beaches and the Electric Train to be created simply to justify their passing through the greenhouse? For the sky to shine during the day and the stars at night solely to allow them to face adventures and defy nightmares? Everything in the greenhouse which opened itself out as heart, everything which rendered itself visible as memory, everything which acted itself out as verb, was also the Firmament, tokens of Essence, if not by nature then by analogy.

"Come."

The stranger kept repeating the self-same invocation. Did desire extinguish creativity? Was the litany necessary to his designs? Had he devised this sonorous expression to fit his fantasy? Was he laying these offerings, this refrain from his hymn, before those filthy hollows and cavities? The Soirée was coming to its close. When I leaned closer to him, he went on to the next verse.

"On top of me."

Driven distracted by the sense of his parts, he was only interested in the Whole insofar as it was the sum of them. The stranger ignored all externality, even the external facts of his own existence. The virgin land had bewitched him. Did he think he would be able to taste a joy stripped of inflexible, inexorable fatality?

The five colours blinded his sight, the five perfumes blotted out all smell, the five sounds numbed his ear, the five savours perverted his taste, the five incantations disordered his consciousness. When the Soirée ended, the stranger did not see the blade as it slit his throat.

THE MAIMED ONE, SECLUDED IN THE Keep with the Sisters, tried to foresee with logic where each of his options might lead him. Though an utter lack of decisiveness characterized his lifeless will, yet nonetheless he lectured his companions, as they bathed him:

"We are living through an age of decadence. This cannot go on much longer. As soon as *He* dies, the little that remains of our ethics, of our very identity, will disappear. Disorder, chaos, and anarchy, beginning here, in the capital, will spread throughout the land. We will have to escape. One must prepare oneself either to flee . . . or to collaborate."

The Maimed One referred to this "He" as though to a figure out of myth or fable. Snatches of an apocryphal hagiography had even reached the Firmament: He, so this version recounted, after eighty years in his mother's womb, had at last been born—with the face and features of an old man. The Maimed One scoffed:

"When I lost my leg He decorated me. In his palace. He was young, a soldier. . . . That was near forty years ago."

Was the Maimed One, guilt-ridden, thinking of his own nature? Forgetting, ignoring, all prior doctrine, system, philosophy? Was the ever present void burying history in the shrouds of amnesia?

"We live looking toward a future with no future."

The Maimed One asked me to call the Sisters "aunt". A sudden transubstantiation had converted me, for them, into "niece".

"Doesn't it make you happy to be with the three of us? You only come to the Keep when you are passing through on your way somewhere else, going out or coming in from the street. You look at us as though we were strangers, or some bodies you had never noticed before . . . at your aunts and me! I am your father!"

In the Park, K—, bowing, paid his reverence to the sequoia. It was hundreds of years old. Then he stood motionless for several minutes before it. Had he forgotten my presence beside him? That the day was dawning? Was he meditating over the reality of the sequoia? Was he worshipping it?

"Everything that exists is worthy of admiration."

In the Firmament I had planted a small tree-stump in the Garden of Illumination. Did the turtles train in *sumo* combat with it? Could reptiles practise that ancient sport?

Had K— divined my thoughts?:

"If one wishes to master *sumo*, technique is not enough. The *sumo* wrestler exhibits the martial artistry of self-forgetfulness."

K— clapped his hands together twice, very slowly, fixedly staring at the tree. Did he feel he was brother to the sequoia? To the sun just budding at the horizon? To the cloud passing overhead? To a drop of water?

"The *sumo* combat I practised in my country is a very brief assault, the intense, sudden crash of two wrestlers. The one who wins is he who can push or throw his adversary out of the ring of sand. He does this by transforming his breathing into concentration, his concentration into energy, and his energy into the infinite domain of time."

After making obeisance to the sequoia K— removed his tunic and put on a loincloth and a brief apron. He enjoyed dressing gaily for the ceremony. When he violently butted into the trunk, the fringe of the apron swayed like tentacles in mute psalm. He performed this morning training session as though it were an exercise of his spiritual power. He threw his great naked backside, his cosmic belly, his almost feminine breasts against the tree. A world of infinitely white flesh clashed against the upright matter sheathed in bark. His mind

was blank, emptied of thought, and yet K—'s energy penetrated, permeated, filled the action.

"The centre of harmony is located two centimetres below
the navel. That is the geometric point where the spiritual and
the physical intersect. There are *sumo* wrestlers who weigh
more than three hundred fifty pounds. I will never achieve
that weight."

Was K— seeking original unconsciousness? Was no thought
to intervene? The strength of his massive body, the grace with
which he assailed the tree, the tension of his muscles, the
relaxation after the earthshaking violence of the shock, were
aspects and forms of beauty. I broke it down into its parts so
that I could better savour it. Were these the various stages on
the road toward the liberation of his self? Toward the immaculate peak of splendour and happiness?

"Three years ago you went away for a week. I had just
arrived here from my country. If you leave again, tell me."

In the Park K— cut mint leaves, daisies, and lantana. He
prepared a lunch for me with them—raw tuna with noodles
made of turnips. He served me in small lacquered boxes. With
one of them I built the first palace-fortress, the Alcázar, in the
spurs of the Vigorous Mountains. Often, a lizard would bask
on top of it when there was sun. Was it sleeping? Did the
lizard believe the sun had created that edifice solely for the
lizard itself? Did it overestimate even the most important
things? Did a god, for lizards, dwindle to no more than a
grammatical fiction?

S— dressed like the model employee of a vigorous, forward-
looking business enterprise. Would he have liked, when he
left off his painting, to wear a ruffled skirt? S— played at being
the epitome of normality:

"Existence reveals evil, suffering, pain."

Was S— referring to inner pain? I somehow saw, guessed,
how unequal reality was to his desires, how crabbed in comparison. Existence, for him, was precarious, illusory, merely
phenomenal, while essence was stable, true, permanent. Did
he want to enter paradise? He yearned after delight, enjoy-

ment. He wanted so much to be loved. Above all, he aspired to strip himself of everything, to return to the inwardness of his essence. He had been enthralled by the Soirée:

"Have you read the newspapers? A woman, described as being very beautiful, very desirable, about twenty years old, has killed a fifty-seven-year-old man in the Cinema by slitting his throat. With a straight razor, a barber's razor."

When a spark leapt in the brazier, for one instant it lit the entire room, and then it disappeared as it fell back into the ashes. S— had resigned himself to being Spark for the most infinitesimal part of a second, a burning flash that flares and then winks out. Did the Soirée represent for him the most intimate secret of his own soul?

"It is a case which interests me enormously! And since I trust neither the newspapers nor the police, I have begun an investigation on my own. I went to the Bar where they sat for a half-hour before they went to the Cinema. They went to the last screening of the evening. There were only about a dozen people in the audience, and yet the two of them went into the last row. In the Bar, she ordered—hot chocolate! I spoke to the waiters."

On occasion S— would ask himself, "What is it that keeps me in this world? What impels me to go from Body to Body?" Hungry for those figures, was he yet sick of appearances? The mechanics of pleasure and the carnal urges of his desires, once translated into acts—did they strike an internal fire? Those acts, those couplings, linked together in a long chain of acts— were they a presage of succeeding incarnations?

"Sometimes, as a youth, I would tell myself, Stop desiring and you will never act again. Today I think that if I renounced the act the desire would disappear. The murderess—that is how I think of her, 'the murderess'—the murderess has taken life during the act, trying to dry up desire once and for all. I must find her. She is an insect of my own species, a butterfly with the forked tail of the flycatcher, my murderous little sister. . . . She is . . . me myself . . . on the road to knowledge."

S—'s rational bent led him to seek an admissible explanation for the mystery of creation. He assumed that nature had two foundations—one good, one evil. Light and darkness. Two antithetical facets which represented the two faces of human existence. And between them lay our feeble forbidden passions, yet neither wrong nor not wrong.

"Three years ago you went on your first . . . and last . . . trip. I took you to P—'s house. He had one foot in the grave, but that brilliant painter's head of his was brimming over with ideas. At least so the news commentators said after he died. A week after you had left."

All the doors to the greenhouse had been boarded over. The only entrance was an opening about halfway up the wall. One reached the opening by way of a steep ladder. Neither the Maimed One, crippled and halt, nor the Sisters, in their obesity, could climb it. Thus the inviolability of the Firmament was preserved. The little entry door was known as the Primordial Threshold. Did insects which had never been outside the greenhouse consider it the door of light, life, and consciousness? Did they imagine that by the grace of a ladder of infinite rungs they might be able to reach the sun?

P— did not live in a city. He dwelt on a peak. A walled peak. The steel door of his Croft opened of its own accord. P—'s face had more wrinkles than S—'s knees. The small screen flickered among his canvasses.

"You spent a week with P—. You locked yourself up alone in his studio in the Croft for seven times seven hours, and all I know is that you watched television. You, who never do that. Forty-nine hours together, a fifteen-year-old girl and an old man ninety-one years old. . . . And his wife, as jealous as she was, never said a word."

It was said that the first pair of serpent-flies in the greenhouse were born inside the stem of a mushroom—a *Boletus castaneus*. They blindly awaited their fate. They were nourished by the dew that collected on the cap. It filtered down to them through the mushroom's porous surface. This pair gave birth to another, which also lived inside the mushroom stem, while the first couple began populating the Firmament, giving rise to all the species of insects. Inside the mushroom stem was there always a pair of serpent-flies which would survive the destruction of the Firmament so as to repopulate it anew?

P— would often say that since his operation he could not impregnate a woman:

"But I manage a normal life in spite of my little infirmities— sex and red wine."

K— had told me to be in the Park to meet him at eight o'clock. Eight o'clock at night, I assumed. An hour later I was still waiting for him. I stretched out on a stone bench. I fell asleep. I dreamt that a cat had curled up on my breast. I woke up. A stranger in a letter-carrier's uniform had his hands on the breasts-of-my-body. Startled, he snatched his hands away. He began to cry heartbrokenly.

"Every corner of the Park has sheltered us. I have kissed her under every tree, I have caressed her in every bed of flowers. . . . Now she refuses to see me again . . ."

The postman was trembling. He began to cry again. What her absence had cropped his memory enlarged. I had never seen K— cry. Were tears a sign of some defect in mortals? A corruption of the soul? Had the union which linked the postman with his beloved separated him finally and for all time from the race of man? Had his passion been transformed into tenderness for himself? Into the weight of pleasure stolen from hard marble fatality?

Why had S— taken me to visit P—? Why did he always have me paint my eyes and lips? Why did he always put lace underwear on me? Why did he draw designs about my navel? Why would he always cloak me in veils, tight bodices, hats? Why did he photograph me in his studio? Why would he fuss so over me as he arranged my hair? And why with elaborate combs and flowers? Did he want to see me stagger under the weight of the tawdry wings of beauty's artifices?

"A woman—would she cry, in my place? . . . at the verge of the abyss of melancholy?"

The postman took me to his apartment. When the door opened, a record player started up. Three orange lightbulbs simultaneously glowed. He showed me two albums of photographs of his beloved and a wooden file-box stuffed with more snapshots. She looked older than he. In almost all the photographs she was *en déshabillée*. Looking at the images of that unclothed body changed his behaviour. Memory and veneration gave way to the vaporous presence of an immediate desire. Probably, through one stage, veneration and desire coexisted in such a way that the postman did not think he was betraying the memory when he undressed. Her spirit materialized through a complex process. His brain with its one hundred trillion nerve cells engendered it, as though his brain were the most wonderfully sophisticated of machines. But what were the rules of this machine?

The postman asked me to put on his lover's dress. White with a tulle sash.

"I am going to do something that no one will believe if you tell them. When I think about . . . Look . . . I'm going to . . ."

He fell onto the bed and concentrated. Did giving, for him, mean relinquishing a part of his fortune in the hope of receiving? Was he preparing a feast at which the meal would be served to him alone? Did these nibbles at pleasure spoil his appetite for eternity? Did his actions seem to him real once more, when he performed them in good conscience? In what region of his brain were his memories locked?

"You are not paying attention. . . . Look at it. . . . Turn around . . . around."

It bobbed about like a sluggish little bell-clapper. Which would present more difficulties—drawing a map of the termite nest in the Firmament or graphically representing the circuits formed by the mail carrier's nerve cells?

"Get on your knees. This way. Facing me. Now, listen. I am going to lie down. I am going to place my buttocks on your thighs and my feet behind you, my left foot to your right and my right foot to your left. Do exactly as I tell you. The way she did. That is why you are dressed in white."

Could the cerebral route which led to excitation ever be translated into mathematical terms?

"Worship it as she did, and then swallow it all."

K— ate certain flowers. He told me the stalk was more flavourful than the petals. For K—, eating was a way of gaining some intuition of his own power and the energy of the universe, of scorning all things improper, of esteeming all things proper. He extracted the juice of some kinds of mushrooms and swallowed it as though it could confer eternal life on him. Did he repay that gift with fervidness? The pressings from the mushrooms induced in him coloured visions, he heard singing, he thought he could fly.

"Do I disgust you?"

The postman lay naked straddling me. His head, at the farthest possible distance from my own, was hidden under a pillow. Were his loins the guest at a banquet, and his head, at a sacrifice? Was he tasting that triumphant splendour which lay between vertigo and darkness? And yet, he went on reciting his meticulous instructions. The performance—the rhythm, the pressure, the position of my right hand, of my left, of my lips, of my knees, of my teeth, of my bosom—had to coincide exactly with that of an inimitable model. The ritual he directed with such precision had three functions—to create in his body a state of hallucination which would give him supreme powers of a magical nature; to exercise, thanks to this magical supremacy, an intemporal power over his body; and to engender delights, sensations capable of making him forget his own existence.

The Soirée, itself omnipotent, took its own way. Like a prince, the postman distributed the *largesse* among the cells of his body. Was he expecting the dull brilliant gleam of gold?, the sparkle of diamond?, the flash of lightning? The glow of light everlasting? The pillow masked his face but not the barely audible, interminably rhyming wheeze, or lament, he emitted. He did not see the blade as it sliced across his throat.

I WOULD SOMETIMES SPEND A LATE AFTER-noon alone in a classroom in the Conservatory. I would listen to the musical message of one stranger interpreted by another. For S——, centuries of gushing spring water and germinating seed could be concentrated into one instant:

"Music is akin to the gift of glossolalia. . . . Tongues of fire descend on men's heads and illuminate the understanding."

The Closet of Fustian was a large steel drum in the greenhouse, hermetically sealed. Into it I poked both the maxims I wrote on cigarette papers and my sanitary napkins. Seven per month. Ninety-one per year. In one woman's lifetime how many would she use? Less than three thousand? Was this number the symbol of ephemerality? My thoughts and my blood imprisoned forever within the Closet of Fustian signified the impenetrable mutuality of life, culture, and death, bundled into one formless unity.

Four million years before the creation of the Firmament, a female with apelike features, on a savannah, went from an arboreal existence to a terrestrial life. With a few oleander leaves she confected a coarse bung which heralded the future sanitary pad. How many millions of those articles had been used by her descendents? As many as the grains of sand along a beach? Was this number an image of eternity still counting, still unfinished?

Two million years before the Firmament, the first female *Homo habilis* saw the light of day. Her speech had only the complexity of that of a two-year-old girl of modern times.

With the long thumbs of her agile hands she made the first fully effective sanitary pad, the first object deliberately manufactured. What impact did this act of creation have on the evolution of the female *Homo habilis?* Did thus commence the awakening of the human spirit? Did the female *Homo habilis* ask herself, "Why do I bleed? What is the meaning of this flux? Who has created me in this fashion? What is my destiny on this savannah?" Her infant intelligence did not allow her to find specific answers to these questions. Did she then invent a maze of mirrors so that she might be able to bear her anguish? And did this introduce witchcraft into her life? And then religion? To her mind came, out of her ancestral memory, images of her foremothers living on all fours in the trees. They did not wear napkins between their legs. She remembered how adopting an upright posture and a bipedal system of locomotion had created the necessity of placing that first compress between her legs. Did it make the female feel more comfortable? Did she remember the remote past with sadness? Had she felt in greater harmony with nature before? Did she ask herself whether she could any longer be happy without sanitary pads? Did she create a myth of the Golden Age? Develop an embryonic theory of ecology? Invent nostalgia? Did grasping at those contradictory emotions refine her intelligence? The preparation of sanitary napkins presupposed the repetition of an action, the elaboration of a custom. Did that, as a consequence, promote the creation by the females of the group of its highest reach of culture? Did this culture forge social links between the females? And did this achievement bring about the fundamental step of food-sharing among the group?

Sixty thousand years before the Firmament, Neanderthal woman buried her compresses after their use. What stages of spiritual evolution did this intelligent action foretell, entail? Did this funerary rite establish the metaphysical concept of time? What ramifications did this discovery have on the life of the group? Female *Homo sapiens,* shortly afterwards, began to bury the dead. Did blood symbolize life to her? Burial, death? What reflexions did this duality inspire in the woman? What interpretations did her religious beliefs suggest to her? Did the fulness of self-possession which she thereby achieved allow her to snatch back from the Final End one throb of reckless hope?

Nine thousand years before the Firmament, woman left off her speculations about the mystery of her flow. She then began a series of phenomenological reflexions about it: How did life come about? What were the causes that brought about a birth? As a result of these introspections a rudimentary agriculture grew up. Human groups began to grow larger. City-states appeared. Barter developed, an economic transaction which grew more and more complex.

Five thousand years before the Firmament, woman began to wish to record the periodicity of her menstrual cycle, so as to ready compresses, note down tardinesses, count absences. She engraved information on clay tablets by means of lines, rectangles, circles, and triangles. Thus she became a bookkeeper of cycles, periods, and blanks. With this was born humanity's first ideographic writing. The first calendars, therefore, were lunar. Were the mainsprings of culture and civilisation, then, forged by the female flux? And was the transformation the result of learned gestures, more and more subtle and sophisticated? Was beauty perseverance?

Would my behaviour in the Firmament, and, as a consequence, the behaviour of all the insects which inhabited it, have been different had I not entombed my sanitary pads in the Closet of Fustian; that is, had I modified the natural conditions of life?

I listened intently in the Conservatory. In the next classroom a stranger was playing the piano. His specific, circumstantial knowledge and his immemorial, racial knowledge came face to face during his interpretation. Was he rehearsing so that when his day came at last, he could show that he was an initiate? I sat alone, listening for errors. When they came, I tasted the pleasure of a revelation not meant for me. Error belonged to a unique musical *genre.* In a concert performed flawlessly, inspiration created the *nuances,* the development, the tone. The music obeyed normative principles which were music's only *raison d'etre*. But the shock of a *faux pas*—was it that the instant's lapse made the sacred immediate by its very absence, or did it evoke the folly and muddle of life? The abstract as over against the unsure, the tentative, the accidental?

K— played a wooden flute. With it he emitted a muted, piercing sound like the melody of a colony of spear-ants. The *motif* made one think of repetition. It reënacted the prodigious memory of insects for learning and combining sound and movement. It suggested the song of the whale, lasting perhaps a half-hour, which the great cetaceans repeat note for note, unerringly, in the deserted nights of the oceans. When I listened to K— I understood why symbolic thought had to have preceded language in the Firmament, because perfection implied sounds undreamt-of by the tongue.

S— rouged my cheeks, the lobes of my ears, my forehead. He drew silver scales on my breasts one by one, a ladybug on my belly, a cock's spurs on my ankles, waves on my neck and throat. He studied my body from inches away, prying into me everywhere. He treated me as though I were merely an individual of a group:

"You are covered with orifices, *mucosa,* wet holes, soft places. What is a woman?"

S— examined me like a doctor, holding a flashlight. Was he disgusted? Envious? Curious? Throughout her life, a woman's uterus held four hundred ova. A man, each time he ejaculated, spewed forth millions of spermatozoa. Would S— have liked to have possessed that uterus which evoked in him such repugnance and terror? Did his very spermatozoa impel him to couple with numerous beings? Or did his dream of possessing, as a woman does, a single ovum every twenty-eight days exhort him to mate with but one single lover? Was he discovering the possibility of a virginal dawn unheralded by the dazzling flare of libertinage?

S— drew a honeybee with its antennae on my lips. Other times he would paint the same zone on my body with an abyss, or a raging pyre, or some remote loveliness frozen in time.

"The murderess has slit another throat. But no one sees the connexion between the two crimes. When will they wake up?"

I was lying on the table. The light touch of his brushes on my body made me drowsy.

"D— has written my uncle. He is to give a party at his castle. Only couples will be allowed to attend. I would like you to go with me."

The caretaker and the porter of the Conservatory discovered me. "What are you doing in a classroom, all by yourself? Are you a student? Who sneaked you in here? How many of you are there? Did you come in to rob the place? To smoke hashish? Are you on drugs? What gang are you with?"

Did man remember more things than the harlequin bedbug? In what region of his memory were his primordial hunting experiences kept locked away? Was hunting an elephant different from hunting a hind? Were the pleasures of the closing net of beaters, the stalking, the chase, fundamentally unlike in the two cases?

The two employees of the Conservatory shared the position of beater. Their venereal past suddenly opened into the clearing of this dark classroom. The presence of prey—me—brought up the memory. They assumed again—pulled from some dark *cache* in their ancestral memory—the role: forgotten gestures, the implacable system which had allowed their forebears to survive. And even to exult: pleasures fitting for solitary bodies.

"We've got to turn her over to the cops."

"At one o'clock in the morning? We can't just leave the Conservatory, just like *that*. And what if some other bitch like this one . . ."

"So I'll take her, and you . . ."

"Tomorrow morning, we can both go. It'll be easier. After work, we'll go by the station."

"Yeah? And what do we do with her in the meantime?"

"I'll take care of that."

"What if she gets away?"

"She won't move an inch."

The caretaker and the porter took me down into the basement of the Conservatory building. The boiler was turned up high. They opened a door to a low, dingy room and threw me onto a pile of wood, sticks, and splints for the heater. Then they locked the door. I began to feel drowsy. I could distantly hear them whispering. Their appetites were sprouting wings and carapaces. In a while the door opened. The caretaker was screaming furiously:

"We've got to give her a lesson!"

"We're not exactly the ones to . . ."

"If not us, then who then?"

"The police . . ."

"The police! . . . This slut thinks she can walk in here and spend the night in the Conservatory like it was a flophouse."

"All right, all right. Calm down. You're getting yourself all heated up. She's not even saying a word."

"What do you expect her to say? What's she got to say for herself? Huh?"

"Well, we're not her judge and jury."

"Didn't you hear what I told you? . . . She'll be back tomorrow . . . with her friends this time. . . . This'll be an opium den in about two days, it'll turn into some cheap cathouse!"

The caretaker was passionately reliving a capture. Did he imagine himself subduing a netted member of some clan of aesthetes? Did the porter's presence, his timidity, spur him on? Did he imagine himself shattering with one powerful blow of his hand a crystal tower of exquisite fragility? Destroying what beneath the level of thought I most centrally *was?* Did treading on what he thought had been created for reverence exalt him, exult him? The boiler so near the two men was making them sweat.

"We've got to strip her."

"Are you nuts?"

"She might try to escape. She can't go out into the street stark naked, no way."

"What if my wife shows up?"

"You're just doing your duty as the porter, like I'm doing mine as the caretaker. We get paid to watch the Conservatory, don't we? To make sure things run smooth, to keep the order, not so some filthy tramp . . ."

They stripped me. Did this man share his ancestors' delight, their glee? Did he know that he was mortal? Did he suffer because of that?

"Where were you born?"

"Who're your folks?"

"Where do you live?"

Did the two men associate their words with concepts and their behaviour with the circumstances that had caused it? As they interrogated me, in the basement of the Conservatory, did the fervour they evidenced betray the structure of myth? Did they identify themselves with reason and justice? As its secular arm, could they peer into hearts as though they themselves were unfettered blood?

"Snotty bitch."

"She couldn't be any quieter."

"'Cause she's making fun of the whole thing. Thinks she's so hot."

"I don't see where you get that."

"We're cockroaches to her, lice. Look how she's looking down her nose at us."

"I'll tell you the truth, I don't see it."

"I'll show her what kind of lice we are."

"What are you going to do?"

"She's got to be punished. So she'll learn her lesson . . . and not try this again."

They exuded nervousness and indecision. I was hardly another human being to them, but could they appreciate what I was? My particular genus? Did they desire to be possessed by the very spirit of vengeance? They imitated it—but disappointedly?, simply from caprice? Were they looking for confession, mercy, and forgiveness? Were they mature enough for this surprising machinery of conscience? Did irrationality hinder them? Was cruelty suddenly springing up in them? Did each fall, each notch downward, awaken new desires?

"Come over here."

The caretaker was sitting in a kitchen chair. He imprisoned me in the vise of his knees.

"Leave her alone, for God's sake."

"I told you, these vipers, you've got to make 'em spit out all the poison they're carrying."

"Don't hurt her. . . . You've got no right."

The caretaker took me by the hair. He pulled my face to his. His eyes—fierce?, frightened?—blazed only inches from mine. Sweat trickled into his eyebrows. Steel gleamed in his false teeth.

"So you think the Conservatory is the Ritz Hotel?"

Could K— have knocked down a wall with his head? Toppled a bull? An elephant? His strength was an art within an art, the burning retasting of tasted experience, the rind and marrow of life. It determined the way in which he identified himself with truth. Was it a source that would never run dry? Did K— dive down into his own mountainous mass of flesh to receive new life?

"You hear me? . . . Stop daydreaming, pay attention to me! . . . What're you thinking about?"

"No need to shout at her like that."

"She's nothing but a dirty little whore."

"She hasn't moved a muscle. She's not making a peep."

"You think she's so sweet and innocent, huh? . . . Naked from the ground up! . . . Showing everything she's got . . . not blinking an eyelash about it, either. Brazen bitch!"

"You were the one that took off her clothes."

"Just so she wouldn't try to get away."

"But so what've you got against her then?"

"She's a tramp. A shameless tramp. She doesn't even care if we see her buck naked as the day she was born."

"Leave her alone, for God's sake."

"She's gotta pay . . . what she owes us."

I had gone to the Conservatory without my purse, without the razor.

Money was sent to the Firmament from the Keep and to K—'s studio from his country. It proved the privilege a predecessor bore to his descendants. It was testimony that by their origin flesh, blood, experience, habit, and fate were allied. Like a child's voice with grandfather's intonations.

"I'll make her . . ."

"Just calm down. You're all worked up."

The caretaker rubbed my face back and forth across his pants.

"What in the world are you doing?"

"Whatever the fuck I feel like. This little whore is getting what she deserves."

Why was it that particular punishment that the caretaker wanted? Was the orifice through which one ate the proper place to introduce the conduit through which one urinated? Did yesterday's man, *Homo habilis,* also demand that same manner of injection? What did it mean? Was it a symbol of the desire to change natural law? Did imagination excite him? Did the caretaker aspire to self-disrespect? Was he attempting to degrade me in the very act of existing? Was he showing by this penetration his animosity toward nature? Could one find, underground, some sense of affection?

Sitting in the chair, the caretaker went on insulting me. Paradoxically, at the same time he was caressing me. The hatred which spewed from his mouth was accompaniment to the tenderness his hands manifested as they touched the breasts-of-my-body. Bent over him, I could see his mud-caked boots ill-concealed by his trousers crumpled at his ankles. Did the dissonance between his hands and his mouth indicate a difference of intensity, or of nature?

The porter, motionless, silent, looked at us.

P—'s cameo was buried in the Firmament under the Banner of the Scribes, covered over with grains of silica. If the gods existed, what were they like? Did they accept the illusory, relative reality which surrounded us? Did men nourish them? Was it that men recognised in them a presage of Essence and, even without having recognised their miracles, made ready offerings to them in advance?

"You take her from that side."

"You're raping her. *I'm* not taking advantage of the situation, not me."

"She's begging for it. . . . Give it to her! . . . That's the way! . . . Hold her real steady. . . . That's it! . . . See, I told you it'd slip right in. . . ."

Was the labour imposed on me by the employees of the Conservatory intended as torture? The activity over my body recalled a skirmish. Was it a symbol of war? An image of conquest? An acting-out of death? My womb and my mouth joined to each of them—did this embody the idea of travail? Was the pendulation impermanence, and why did it take the form of such a short, quick cycle? Were the contrasted rhythms, attitudes, and words of the two men contending? Coming to agreement? Did buried concepts appear in the swaying balance? In the inevitable oblivion into which they would fall?

The first time, they both finished at almost the same instant. The caretaker threw me to the floor. He advised the porter:

"Wash over there, at the faucet . . . these wildcats are capable of even having acid inside. . . . Their mouths're okay, but there . . ."

K— stated that infinity was equal to zero. One plus one—how many times did that not add to two but to another figure which, qualitatively, had nothing whatever to do with the two units?

After repeated ablutions the cycle of attacks continued, like the cycle of ruin and discord. Then they fell to the ground. Faint with weakness? Sated? Exhausted? The caretaker snored. But I had gone out without P—'s razor.

L OCKED SNUGLY WITHIN THE GREEN-house, I often meditated on suffering, on the origins of suffering, on the way to ease suffering, and on the way to achieve suffering. K— would say that a paradise did exist:

"Here and now."

At the age of thirteen K— was chosen. He entered a stable of *sumo* wrestlers in his country.

"You and I now make a stable, even though you are not a wrestler."

During his painful initiation K— came to accept the most rigorous discipline. He also learned to breathe.

"Thanks to his mastery of breath, the human being is an image of creation. I respire with the universe. The muted balance of its music fills me to overflowing."

When in the morning K— would sprinkle the foot of the sequoia with handfuls of salt, as purification, did he lament having left his land? Did he feel he had abandoned his destiny as a *sumo* wrestler, which would have led him to fortune and glory? He portioned his universe of flesh into two halves as he threw his legs far out to each side—earth-splitting stomps. His strength and agility were combined in this time of fervour. His equilibrium was enclosed in a sheath of silence. But at the same time he could hear the music of his respiration, the deep breaths of his life, the energy emanating from his body, permeating and filling him. He embraced the universe and himself.

"The action of my hands, my shoulders, my forehead, when

I throw myself against the sequoia, is the extension of my breath."

K— became fluid, tenuous, impalpable as the breeze. Idea engendered him out of seaspray. A snowflake could have changed his weight.

K— ate to imagine, to meditate, to contemplate. He set out in open, varnished cases—red parallelopipeds with stars or ivory-coloured rhombuses—green mustard in the shape of conical thimbles, noodles braided into Möbius strips. He used virtually transparent porcelain cups, plates like ships sailing over the table, spheres cut in two at their bases by scimitars, chopsticks for shredding eternity. Rigour and beauty.

S— ate to innovate, to surprise, to startle. Lace napkins coquetted beside a prodigal brigade of goblets and chalices. A table set for the rotogravures, a party, some country inn. No dish came from where one would have thought. Truffles, biscuits, tea allowed voyages, dreams through an imaginary geography. Discoveries and the wonders of far-distant flavours, hushed and silent, passed by. If one expected rice, seed-spores appeared. If one were trusting in white, green would spring forth. He cooked to disorient my mind and give solace to my mouth. So that I would let myself be carried away by melancholy, unconsciousness, abandon. So that the taste of an ecstasy would taint my appetite with everlastingness.

In the Keep, at midnight, the Sisters, one after another, would sally out against the refrigerator. After serving the Maimed One at the long ceremonial of dinner, and then putting him to bed, they embarked on their culinary expeditions. Like ravaging animals. Did hunger so brutally gnaw at them? Was transgression the precondition of their gluttonous feasts? An impulse of supernatural origin guided them in their sieges against the refrigerator. Were they acting out a myth? Were they directing an orchestra without music or audience?

The Sisters observed every rule of extravagance in their gorging. They preferred the gross, the disgusting, the detestable. Implacably, invariably. As between a filet with wild morels and truffles and leftover macaroni from a package, they would choose the macaroni. They slathered it with mayonnaise. From a jar. Just taken out of the refrigerator, giving off cold steam.

Were they hungry for food or for maceration? Was it appetite or anguish? The two Sisters afforded a delicate spectacle of affliction. Only the vile attracted them.

Cold things enchanted them. The Sisters elevated the esoteric cult of Frozen Foods, practised by children and adolescents, to the height of veneration. They would lick, suck, slurp, gnaw at frozen potatoes sliced in strips as though they were sticks of ice cream. If they discovered a soup through whose frozen surface glacial croutons peeked, they would not eat it with a spoon, they would employ a hammer and chisel. They would carve out icebergs of soup. They would smack as the arctic blocks melted on their palates, they would crunch them drunkenly, and soon they would be soaked and wet as though from the sobbed-out tears of glowworms plunged into darkness by desolation.

Did the Sisters aspire to avoid suffering? Did they imagine that it was not inherent in all existence? Did they long for serenity as the final product, the end, the result of the internal hurly-burly of their entrails? Did they yearn to die as martyrs of a sect of ingurgitators, foundering in a privy retreat? Did they invent laws so as to escape them? Did they realise that their lives had come to revolve about the brief convulsion of a subordinate delight?

Did K— invent evidence at their expense?

"It is possible to not eat. It is best to not feel hunger. Certain men during an early stage of their life copulated like animals. Pleasure arose from woman's humiliation. At a second stage they learned certain techniques of control to please her. The coupling did not conclude with an ejaculation. They were able, at the moment the ejaculation was about to occur, to aspirate it, to raise it up into the cranial temples, so that it might bedew their heads. In the third stage, after having achieved mastery over ejaculation, they conquered desire.

They no longer, ever, felt hunger. The path is not extinction, but illumination."

The Sisters needed chocolate to solve their sentimental problems. They needed it when they had been made to cry. Did chocolate contain amphetamines? Opium? Cocaine? Did it flush away anger more efficaciously than an inhalation of model-aeroplane glue? Than the oblivion of forgetfulness itself?

They drank condensed milk from its container with their thick naked lips, bowls of cream with soup spoons. They would put plastic bottles of fruit juice into the freezer and take them out transformed into icicles. They would flay them of their plastic skins with scissors and suck on the huge blocks of ice. They perfumed them with melted lard and sprinkled them with grated cheese.

So that they could go on eating in bed without the Maimed One's being aware of it, the Sisters would stuff slices of salami into the pockets of their nightdresses. As well as scoopsful of *croissants, mallorcas, beignets,* and rolls. Unwrapped. They would eat boiled potatoes still in the skin, figs with their rind, hard-boiled eggs shell and all, shrimps whole. They ate spinach with *baklava,* a *potage* of ham and beans with frozen raspberries. They gulped down herrings with layer cakes, *yoghurt* with Spanish sausage, tripes with strawberry milkshakes.

As the Sisters surfeited, did the world once more return to uninterpretable fable? A parable laden with prodigies and wonders and proof against magic spells? Did they grow to have a clearer and clearer idea of God? Was he, for them, a fattened sow? How could humanity represent that in the illustrations for communion texts?

When morning came, the two of them would be eating with their hands beslimed with sauces. They used their hands like ladles, like shovels. They would sit astride a kitchen chair before the open door of the refrigerator. They would finally eat the packages, dishes, delicacies wrapped in paper. Did the Sow, like the purest element between the spheres of the sun and the fixed stars, appear to them at the end of the feast, radiant, above the freezer, surrounded by cherub-sucklings?

Did the Soirées stun S—? Obsess him? Wall him into his own timid and wavering self-admissions?:

"Have you read the description of the murderess that the press has managed to put together?"

Did S— fully know virility because he preferred the feminine?:

"I would like to be the world's valley."

In the greenhouse favour was a resource unequally meted out among the individuals of an insect species. Among the ants were recognised queens and slaves, warriors and labourers. Among the warriors there existed the explorers and the defenders. Among the explorers, *avant-garde* scouts and rearguard escorts. Among the *avant-garde,* those of the first line and those of the next lines back. Why didn't the Maimed One establish a hierarchy among the Sisters?

Curiosity, wholly integral in its certainty, hounded, besieged S—:

"If you only knew how much that young woman interests me! In my mind's eye she walks along the street and allows herself to be mounted by a stranger who might be her grandfather . . . and slits his throat an hour later! She must be insatiable! She is a cicada, like I am, or better yet a rhinoceros scarab. She has just killed a postman with the same razor."

Sometimes, when I bent over, I had the sense of being erect; when I was empty, of being full. I would be shaken by irresolution; time escaped me. For S— all was absurd:

"However much femininity I adopt . . . I can only be a copy of a copy. You possess the spontaneity of unity."

Did S— assume that by not behaving according to the norms one lost one's unity? Did his unquenchable bitterness squeeze him in a vise of exactitude?:

"I have been to see the postman's apartment. A neighbour with the keys permitted me to visit it. It let me understand so many things!"

Lying on the straw mat in the Firmament, I imagined a State

like the Keep, with its same spirit but extended across a continent, ruled by a Maimed One who approved, encouraged, and demanded the removal, at the age of fifteen years, of the right leg of every inhabitant. He would represent and lead a society of millions of human beings, in which every citizen would have the serene conviction that the supreme good was achieved at that moment of mutilation. They would think that God desired that amputation and that the laws of ethics and of history decreed it. *Concerti,* hymns, would be composed to sing forth this rule of conduct. Lyric and epic literature would justify this moral code. The most thoughtful and intelligent men and women would write essays in celebration of it. Scientists would analyse the ablation and affirm that amputation was the practical consequence of wisdom.

K— expressed the opinion that it was the unreal body that committed errors. Did he dwell in a city of unreal bodies? Of mistaken pleasures? Of a confused present? Of eternal shudders and burning chills?

The porter of the Conservatory came out to speak to me as I passed:

"I feel so terrible about what we did with you in the basement! But it wasn't my fault. The caretaker is the one that's a pig. I don't know how I could've lost my head that way . . ."

I withdrew slowly, impassively, from the evening. I admired the excellence of the moment. I contemplated the harmony between the sky and a ringdove hopping along the sidewalk. They seemed, nonetheless, to form part of an incredibly fertile, uninterrupted chaos.

"My friend—the caretaker—all he thinks about is . . . whoring around. He even wants to . . . again, in the Conservatory. I mean, I've had to stop him. I don't want him to ever touch you again. Or even see you. You know what? Since that night I've never stopped thinking about you . . . all the time. . . . I've been dying to see you again. I was afraid you were furious at us. . . . And you'd have had every right to be, too. When I look at you I get goosebumps on the back of my neck. The way you look at me! So sweet! I feel sweet about you, too.

Really, really. More than you'd ever imagine. I'll tell you how much—just looking at you makes me feel better than what we did in the basement did. . . . If the caretaker bothers you, you let me know. I'll crack his skull for him."

The caretaker followed me to the Park. He finally faced me there.

"What are you doing around here? . . . You remember . . . you still remember? . . . We had quite a time in the basement, didn't we? . . . Even if the porter is a first-class snivelling romantic jerk . . . I'm the one you like . . . aren't I? . . . Whenever you want it . . . some other night . . . I'll be ready for you. . . . Plus, I got some pot. . . . A friend of mine just happened to give me a little stash the other day. . . . Plus I've got a movie projector in my apartment . . . and some porno flicks . . . the hottest stuff money can buy . . . hardcore stuff . . . everything . . . I've got a load here for you. . . . Here, just feel this . . ."

Sprawled on the *tatami* under the glass panes of the greenhouse, I could hear only my breathing and my spirit. Not a single convulsion remained. The universe turned. The world fell into tune, into infinity. I could see a blade of grass quivering on a star. My body was floating in space. I could feel the five senses, the five planets, the five sounds, the five vowels. The five colours appeared: red, white, blue, yellow, and green. They irradiated everything. An immaculate light flooded me—tremulous, unbounded, and mine.

An external circle surrounded me like a barrier of fire.

HOW COULD I ARRANGE FOR THE caretaker and the porter to experience and, together, conclude a Soirée with me and P—'s blade? K— understood my yearning as though I had mentally communicated it:

"Imagine two hornets. Suppose that you were to tie one of each of their legs together with a thread, and then that they were to try to fly away. When they realised that they couldn't, they would each become angry and attack the other. Both would assume that the other one was restraining his freedom."

A hunt without hunter. Was this a parable? A lesson? K— was not afraid of, was not put off by, the idea of pouring a flood of consolation on an urgent need.

"The two hornets would mutually destroy each other. The winner, dragged down by the weight, would be anchored to the ground. He would die slowly as food for lyncher-ants and necrophages."

The Maimed One and the Sisters lived Decadence as though it were part of their very biographies. They knew that health carried in itself the seeds of sickness and death, as spring carried those of winter:

"*He* is dying. I give him no more than two months. And then . . . the curtain falls. Time has slowly destroyed us all."

The Maimed One shuddered thinking of His death, as though he almost desired it. He heard in hoarse throats the sound of the rapid approach of chaos.

When I went into the street, the porter from the Conservatory was waiting for me a second time. He argued, with no flush of fright, fear, or embarrassment, the defence of compassion:

"Humiliate me if you want to. Hurt me. Spit on me. Insult me. . . . But don't do the worst thing—don't stand there without saying a word, like you did the other day. I want to hear your voice. I want to know that you forgive me for what we did with you in the basement. It was rape. . . . I'll never have God's forgiveness, but at least if you . . ."

The porter stopped me in the middle of the street. He seized my wrists. He looked at me. He stood a few moments without speaking. I contemplated his drab brown eyes. I thought, The spirit is nourished on all the cells of the body.

"You look at me so sweetly!"

The Firmament, in its impenetrable wisdom, did not constitute a logical proposition. It expressed itself by way of incommunicable experience which could not in the least be rationally deduced. What message was locked in my eyes? And in those of a sun spider? And in the silence crawling out of the soul?

The Maimed One and the Sisters vegetated, recluses. Did they yearn to be transformed into larvae? Into nymphs? Into sphinx moths? They had ceased to go out on Sunday mornings.

"The times are going to change. One has to adapt . . . and . . . why not? . . . maybe even collaborate!"

The three of them pooled their memories and stirred them all together with fears, phobias, terrors. The stew of memories and fears gave them a fertile imagination. They supposed that the frays and skirmishes of the past, the wars of yesterday, would engender horrible vengeance:

"They will come to get us."

The Maimed One was heard to forgive for the first time in his life those who had shot his leg off.

"Take the trunks up to the greenhouse."

Take them up or bury them? Was he wishing that his past be raised up into heaven? Why ensepulchre it in so high a place? The cabin trunks filled with uniforms would form constellations in the Firmament. The greenhouse became exalted in the Maimed One's fantasies, it rose from mundane to celestial, from ash to live coals, from tortured desire to burning action.

"You look at me with so much love!"

The porter sailed between two rocks: that of defining nothing and that of not knowing or understanding his experiences:

"You are a torment to me."

Were all things pain? Actually or potentially?

P—, now almost deaf, took refuge in his categories. Mundane noise did not reach his crystal asylum with its lunar rocks and dusty boundaries. The steel door of his Croft was erected over a paper *chimera*. P— contemplated me with eyes so myopic that I might have been some inaccessible philosophy incarnated in a feminine body. We spent those seven evenings in his studio when I was fifteen years old like two dragonflies hypnotised by the glow of the television screen.

The porter from the Conservatory, far above rapture, the memory of that night underground, felt, stabbingly, a nostalgia for happiness:

"When I'm with you . . . even if you never even look at me . . . I'm crazy with happiness."

The porter and the caretaker had wanted to humiliate me. Did that degradation allow them to scale the heights of delirium? Was orgasm as mysterious as it seemed? Did it even have a concrete reality? When their muscles entered my body were their thoughts inverted? Did their heads touch the feet of knowledge? Did anguish surround their pleasures?

Other women gave birth like slugs in the rose garden. That is why men mounted them. Had these two men penetrated me only to transform me into a larva paralysed by the prick of a specimen-pin? Did they know I would not give birth? Were they thirsty for pleasure? Was the thirst unquenchable? Was it a thirst to exist? To endure? Instinct planted its flag on the shore of the land of decomposition. Frenziedly? Beneath the veil of automatic actions was discovered the web of secretions and external excretions. If P—'s gift had been with me, the Soirée at the Conservatory, with the caretaker and the porter, would have concluded without their ever awakening.

"I dream about you. You're my whole life. Let me come see you sometime."

Once the porter had come to know the surfeit of pleasure, did he now burn to know the cloying surfeiting of love? Could the process ever be reversed? Were the froths of love and pleasure linked one inside the other? Were they a vicious circle? The porter extracted affection from the mass of information stored in his memory during that night in the basement. Those data, held in the form of symbols and words, composed a sketch, a *maquette*. Could he himself ever correct that map? Change his, its concepts? Did he recreate the scene in the basement and imagine future events?

"Don't you get me? . . . I love you!"

The porter pulled from among the stimuli arriving in his mind those which would lead his affections. In the passion of affliction, he stood face to face with emotion.

"I love you with all my heart!"

The porter chose those memories which were emotionally most convenient for him. Sublimated memory and the assaults of fondness constituted his unconscious thought. Did he identify with the physical foundations of his memory and his love? In what part of his body were they located? Could he have categorically excluded his groin? His brain? His eyes? His heart? His hands?

"The man you saw—that wasn't *me*. For me, always, I've tried . . . The most important thing in the world for me is not to steal, not to kill, not to lie, not to get drunk, and not to run around with other women."

The porter believed in the morality of the five self-denials. But he dreamt of its collapse. What part had he assigned me in the destruction? Was he seeking, only?, the welfare of his body?

I would only open the Medicine Cabinet in the Firmament

to put in my jars of creams and unguents. I prepared the potions with the ashes of excreta of my body that I burned and mixed with powder. They contained in themselves an image of the process which leads to the decay of energy, to the ineluctable increase of disorder.

S— dreamt as well:

"The murderess understands that her body is for the first man that comes along at night. She only kills by night. The sun, daylight, prevent her from celebrating her ritual."

S— intuited that Decadence was a part of the present. The Maimed One was frightened by this fall into disorder. S— valued its positive aspects. Every physical or mental process entailed an acceleration of the disturbance. S— avidly, enviously observed this:

"The two victims, the old man in the Cinema and the postman, had an orgasm before they died. The coroner has just announced it. At last the police will have to establish a link between the two murders."

How could one weigh in a balance with any precision using false units of measurement? When personal features were changed, was the individual transformed? Could a flock of toothless particulars gradually fade into substance?

"They say the murderess must be about twenty-two years old, although she looks twenty. I am convinced she is eighteen."

S— snuffled out the underground treasure:

"The murderess excites and kills. She is a woman who can only be understood by a man who dreams of being a woman himself. I have been to the Cinema. I have seen the bloodstain on the carpet in the last row. I sat in the same seat she sat in. In the dark . . . I became her. A female ant-lion readying herself to spring and kill the male."

In the Firmament, after the nuptial flight, the queen ant did not kill the male. He would fall to the ground, there to die a bit later, like a vagrant, tired to exhaustion, with no nest to sleep in, prey of every ravaging insect in the greenhouse.

K— would often say that he was following the path of the gods. He could not conquer the sovereign order of the infinite.

"You and I together make a stable."

What a tumult there was in the nest on those September mornings when the queen ant would make her one and only flight! The worker-ants would excitedly scurry back and forth. They thronged to the orifice at the entrance to the nest. They put one last bite of food into the queen's mouth, a *viaticum* for the bridal journey.

When K—, shoeless and almost naked, trained before the sequoia, did he feel he was a pharaoh-ant? A housefly? A mayfly? A green peach-louse? A bumblebee? A soldier-mosquito?

The queen ant would climb up onto a leaf of grass. Her antennae would hum and quiver. Suddenly she would lift away from the earth and fly. For the first time in her life she would rend the air with her body. She would rise above the ground shining like a bubble of mercury, like the round indecipherable secret sign of fate.

K— would walk with me along the avenue, swinging from side to side under the trees. I would occupy first the right and then the left hemisphere of the world. The spirituality contained in his cosmic body drew the attention of other strollers.

"The chameleon may change, but not the background."

The queen ant would be met by the male in the air. They would glide along together for hours.

K— and I would come to the fountain. Automobiles would revolve around us. K— would peer over the fountain's lip and shout:

"Me!"

When the aerial embrace was done, the queen and the male returned to earth. The male to die. The queen would immediately seek out an opening in the ground, under a stone or a clump of grass.

K— placed his hands on the water of the fountain. Was he meditating?:

"Water is the first element. It produces life, which flows."

Hidden in her own dry well, the queen ant, standing on four of her legs, would pull off her wings. She would never fly again. From that moment on, she would live the twelve or twenty years of the rest of her existence completely buried and walled about. Did she aspire to become familiar with death? Her eggs like infinite grains of sand rust-pitted and corroded by what they meant—did they demonstrate to her the dangers and the menaces of procreation? Could she not stand the dazzle of the light?

The porter from the Conservatory sought the shadows. He pleaded:

"Love me!"

Could the miserable porter guess the connexion between effects and causes? Did he truly think he understood how birth entailed death? How the senses determined the object perceived? How sensations conditioned affect, value?

In the Firmament yellow light emanated from the earth and green light from the air that surrounded me, but infinite light illuminated the lamp, the flame, the fire, and death—a lighthouse guarding over a space in which that purest thing would never fail.

Mutilated, walled in, and mother, the queen ant became the image of sepulture; resurrection, the image of affliction; the two hornets with their legs bound together by a single thread, the image of expiation.

In the fireplace of the Firmament I would burn my hair, my fatted sweat, the mucus from my nose, my excrement. Everything disappeared.

My woman's body did not give life. I was The End.

THE CARETAKER THOUGHT IT WAS HE who had chosen to see me. The butterfly of death elected its itinerary, too, when it flitted from flower to flower. The caretaker had eluded P—'s gift but was still an excellent candidate for it. His initiative, with its bloody fingers, was tracing the unhappy twists and turns that led to his own fate.

"You've eaten up his brain! And I can't stand it. He's my friend!"

The caretaker thought that he had sought me out and found me. As though a magician had thought endless playing cards magically sprang from his fingers. What did he have to tell me? Did all decisions arise as mirages?

"If you don't leave him alone, I'm telling you, this is going to end up pretty ugly . . ."

In the greenhouse male three-barred scarabs struggled for domination of the females. The male was willing to lose his potency in exchange for mating with several females. And the female, to forgo the benefits conferred on her by other unions so long as she might mate with only one male. Conflicts and tensions hobbled the normal evolution of the species.

"I know you've been with the porter. And you've got him as in love as some young kid, you whore! This wipes out everything I told you the other night. No joints and no nice porno movies for you. You come to my house and we'll have a serious talk about this. You make me sick."

S— scorned his uncle:

"He's a penny-pinching tightwad."

For S——, his uncle had fire and money. He was constantly going from one orbit to another. He reflected back the light he sought and bathed in, and he collected the banknotes of his fortune on a continent with no butterflies, no wings, no lovers' lanes, no transparence.

"He buys and sells painters. But he won't even answer letters. I am his nephew!"

S—— pictured each canvas that passed through his uncle's hands slowly metamorphosing into excrement.

"He thinks he can bestow immortality. But he denies it to me. He only uses me as a decorative touch at his parties."

His uncle—did he know the points of concordance, of relationship, of similarity, between fortune and glory? Between the body we drag along and the clouds in the sky? Between skin and a tiny pebble? Between flight and the breeze? Between eminence and affliction?

"And imagine, P—— wrote him a letter after your visit. To *him,* and not to talk about the sales of his paintings—about *you.* It must surely have been P——'s last handwritten text. His last words, sent to a *dealer*—my uncle. As though ethics and business were married."

"Aren't they closely related?"

"Really, my uncle has never tried to give an artist back his own balance, but rather to upset that balance, to make the artist renounce his own self. My uncle transforms the painter from an artist into a printing press for gorgeous banknotes."

Did P—— recognise the insubstantiality of all created things?:

"One has to kill modern art. . . . Enough! No? Everything has been said."

P—— would turn off the television and pick up his brushes.

The painters of the Firmament—did they escape this melancholy? The old paintings disposed one behind another—were they the accumulated decoration of the theatre of the world? The painted last dying moments with their mute pain and grief reflecting the live shadows and darkness?

S—— would ask me what I had done with P—— three years

earlier, how I had spent those seven evenings with him in his Croft.

"I have managed to discover that the murderess is a suave, sophisticated woman with a bewitching gaze. A waiter told me she listens as though she were enchanted. That she's very attractive. A girl from a good family—a fox from the top of the hill, he said."

Was body impure? Were close attachments sources of terrible distress for S—?

"The murderess's head functions like mine does. What I lack is her heart. If I were brave enough to kill the man who desired me I would do it with a razor too."

Sometimes I woke up in emptiness. I couldn't find my thought. On occasion emotion was so profound that I managed not to think of anything.

"Both times she has killed in the same way. The first time she acted perfectly openly, in the Bar. I haven't been able to find any witnesses to the night of the second murder. But I haven't given up all hope."

When I would awake, my thought would suddenly be set in motion. It was continually nourished on something new, as when dawn sank into day, for example.

S— could suddenly, becoming almost a flower, stretch, grow, and cast his head upward:

"If I had been a woman, and had been in the Cinema . . . In spite of being a man, I have, when I wish, the five elements of femininity: I can exhibit the physical appearance of a woman, her emotional sensitivity, and her ability at classification, I am able to reconcile the energies of the subconscious and the unconscious, and I possess the segregating power. I can organise my entire life like that of a woman, around two centres of interest: the individual and the circumstances."

When I awoke in the greenhouse I would gaze at myself in the mirror. I would see my image and that of the rest of things. The reflexion of all things and of the mountains. Scintillations like bubbles in wine.

The caretaker was feverishly waiting. But what was "waiting" for him? The frothy pomp of two waves crashing together?

"I'm talking to you, so you just better listen. I've had enough of you being off in another world, like none of this had anything to do with you."

Did there exist some antagonism between desire and concord? Between sexual ardour and group harmony? Did ants in the greenhouse form the most stable society in the Firmament because the females in the nest were the active, clever, asexual majority and the males a tiny parasitic group, slow, clumsy, and passive, which only took to action for a few brief moments of their life, on the day of their death outside the nest?

The caretaker examined my body-bounded-by-my-skin. From my ankles to the tips of my hair, his gaze tasted the diverse impure ingredients:

"You're a whore from head to toe. Look how you move. Look at that . . . that's how you've driven the porter crazy. But that's enough of turning on every man that passes by!"

Why were the two sexes so distinct? Why did two sexes exist and not four, or seven? Why were the male and female anatomies so different? Was body spirit? And the two together, courtship, betrothal?

"I could slap you . . . and I ought to do it."

Aggressiveness—did it arise as an artifice of courtship? Why did the females of the least intelligent species of insects mechanically go through the motions of placation, timidity? So as to select out the best male possible? Prudent and ambiguous retorts—were they invariably destined to provoke new aggressions from the male, with the aim of finding out the best consort?

"What did you do with the porter the other day that he's so gaga? How many times did you clean his pipes for him, you nympho? It was me that . . ."

What privileges did aggression concede? The caretaker looked at me with so much desire that desire became his very breathing:

"You're a whore, that's what you are."

Did he ever consider that in my body there were skin, bones, flesh, teeth, lungs, tendons, saliva, snot, urine, tears, fat, excrement, pus, and blood? Treasured-up, cached secrets minted in shudders and chills?

"Stop looking at me that way. I'm not falling into your trap."

Fury was an element aerial, earthly, and wet. But the caretaker's body, its fate now decided, burned. Attacking thrilled him. To tame his imagination he invented scenes that he thought were vile:

"I can see you on all fours getting it dog-style from the porter, all over the room. You little pig! You're gonna tell me all about it. Swallowing every drop of it, like you did in the Conservatory. Look at me—it gives me goosebumps just to think about it."

Intuition could only define imaginary situations. The caretaker's jealousy—did it take in memory as well? Was it thanks to that jealousy that he reached his life's fulfilment? Was the mission of this jealousy to intimidate? To attract? Or to destroy? The male weaver-moth in the greenhouse remained coupled to the female, after transferring his sperm to her, for another full hour. Did he hold her out of jealousy? To ward off the competition? To keep some other male from displacing him? Was jealousy a derangement of imagination? Did it sparkle and gleam like butterflies of fire among the branches and leaves of doubt?

"You sleep with the first man that comes along. . . . Have you no shame? I didn't have to push you very hard in the Conservatory. The second I put your mouth within distance . . . like it was the most natural thing in the world . . . you didn't say no to a thing. An army could've had you that night. It's all the same to you. And that poor kid, crazy about you. . . . You're eating him alive . . . the porter. . . . I can't let you. . . . I forbid you to . . ."

In the greenhouse not even twin insects were identical. There were not so many as two molecules absolutely the same.

Each distinct plane of existence corresponded to an internal process. Infinite space was inhabited by infinities of worlds. In jealousy, space constricted. It was the time of involution, of extinction, of shattered impulses, of delirium enclosed in a single instant. Jealousy behaved like a memory which did not retain but rather eliminated. The caretaker exhaled his complaints:

"Stop looking at me like that. With those goo-goo eyes. Like you were in love with me, hah! Like you were so bloody sweet and pure. You know why you never say anything? Because all you'd say would be idiotic common vulgar low-class stupidities. You've figured out how to trick men with your eyes, with that sweet, innocent virgin's look of yours you put on like a Halloween mask. You're a viper. But you're not gonna hypnotize me like some stupid chicken. I'm not the porter. You know something? Ever since I found out you've fucked up his head this way, I wish I hadn't had you in the basement. You don't deserve it."

The queens of the dwarf termites in the greenhouse laid an egg every two seconds. Day and night. For weeks, months, years they gave birth, indefatigably, infinitely producing death thereby. Suffering from the two ills of excitation and lack of discernment, they lived eternally producing from the extruded eggs offspring inevitably to die as dry slough. Did they ever wonder whether life were reality? Or a rough jolt towards fable?

S— painted grasshoppers on my breasts, the wings of an oriental butterfly in my armpits, and scorpion pincers on my legs:

"What if I should hold myself aloof from . . . pleasure? If I should decide that from this day onward it should be a matter of indifference to me? If I should cease to locate exaltation at the level of my loins?"

As S— was speaking to me he was painting around my navel the eye of a falcon-moth.

"I could easily renounce happiness and its nasty concomitants. Even its opposite. I could arrive at spiritual self-sufficiency, feeling neither joy nor pain. I could be pure impassivity."

The brushes rounded my eye sockets. S— aspired to emptied thought, silence, shadow, rotation, absolute flux, the vibration of absence and emptiness in impalpable abandon:

"I shut off, while I paint you, all emotional and reflective activity. I empty my spirit of all memory, of all content whatever."

On occasion my empty consciousness reminded me of the infinite. I could perceive my thought beside me. Like a river. I watched it flow past. At last the river would halt. I would see nothing. The caretaker woke me up:

"How long are you going to make fools of us? You think you're so . . . just because . . . you think you've got some kind of rights over us. I can't stand the porter making dates with you. He's sick, I mean the guy's been mentally ill since he saw you the other day. What did you do to him?"

My body was a battlefield I was imprisoned in like a cricket in his cricket-cage. How could one avoid corporeal torments?

"You're getting me as hot as a stallion in rut. The way you swing your ass around all over the place would make a saint horny, and I'm no saint. In spite of everything, you do something awful to me."

Four hours earlier I had walked through the Keep. The Maimed One was lying on a wicker *chaise longue* with his eyes closed. The elder Sister was shaving him. The younger was washing his foot in a pan of warm water. His arms and hands drooped towards the floor. Sunlight was pouring over him.

"A sunbath each morning . . . and my body can stand another day of this decadence engraved in steel."

K— wrote my name in ideograms. He said that "origin" was the same as "book", "sword", and "strength". Therefore the ideograms for the four words were identical. When he traced out the symbols which composed my name, did he capture me? Did he strip naked my face, my lips, my little hops of joy, the trembling of my griefs?

K— and I bathed each other three times in his studio. In

turn we washed each other with soap, in the shower. Then we both sat in a large wooden washtub. The water was almost boiling. K— intoned his thanksgiving. He said that we were purifying ourselves so as to find our centre of gravity, our equilibrium. The first time he invited me to a bath was the morning after the Soirée in the Cinema.

For the caretaker life was all dissonance, disequilibrium:

"I don't know how I'll ever control myself. I'm about to bust. Who ever taught you to turn men on that way? . . . I could die, I want you so much."

On the Hearth of Allusion in the greenhouse the sticks of wood which fed the fire were consumed in the process. Extinction obeyed this rule, always. What was I to the caretaker? A medicine to be taken to expel the disease and then, taken, to be passed, in the form of exudation or sperm? Or of unanswerable rebuffs like slaps in the face?

"I'm so horny . . . I've even got this pain, here, that's . . . I think I'm going crazy. . . ."

When I returned to the Firmament the Flag of Discipline was planted in the earth exactly midway between the waters of the Vat and the fires of the Hearth. This represented the ideal world. But the universe beyond the walls was composed of a system of elements just at the verge of decomposition. It was ordered by a sensory model which was just barely at the edge of the insensible: rapid, weighty, bitter, unquiet, amidst broken, torn, and shattered glooms.

"I'm like a mad dog for you."

I thought about the caretaker and the porter. I meditated on the parable of the hornets tied together by a thread. After he had told it to me, K— had written on a cigarette paper:

"To feel thirst, one must first have quenched it."

FOR S— THE PRESTIGE ENJOYED BY THE imagination made it an almost intemporal organic unit. It offered victory in the labyrinth.

"I received a telephone call from my uncle. D— is to give the party on Monday in the Castle. We are invited. I must buy clothes for you . . . we'll go together, tomorrow. It will be smashing—how to describe it to you? Imagine a sect of people who have everything, who have been everywhere and done it all, and who know that there is nothing more to be known. And those people want to spend one unforgettable evening."

In the Firmament's past, councils, assemblies, and congresses took place. Motions were made and resolutions adopted which came finally to me in imperfect or perhaps legendary states. Schisms formed. And these gave rise to sects. The Prerogative schism permitted the creation of a renovative concept of the Firmament which clarified and transfigured ancestral notions. But was it truly compatible with traditional thinking? Paradoxically this reformative schism produced as an unexpected consequence a deepening of the study of the first myths-of-origin of the Firmament. It presupposed that the arrival of velvet ants, of ephemerids, of red spiders, of certain mosquitos, of the death-watch beetle, of flags, family, photographs, of flies, had brought about a complex situation richer in hypotheses than in certainties.

A unity was forged which took into account schism, heterodoxy, and orthodoxy, so as to signal the decisive importance of the world outside the greenhouse walls: Keep, Fountain,

Maimed One, Sisters. This universe never ceased to have an influence over the very physical structure of the greenhouse.

For S— fabulation was a constant of human weakness. It showed the general inclination for the marvellous, it served as a kind of sweet but forceful instrument for spasmodic and ephemeral jolts:

"D— says that they shall live the intensest hours of their lives in the Castle. It's a hook to snare couples who have tried everything and are bored by it all . . . but who still want to think that somewhere, something must exist that will shock, stun, or startle them, or even drive them to delirium."

The porter, in the brute beast's eternal present he inhabited, neither reasoned nor reflected:

"It's you? . . . Is it true? . . . Am I dreaming? . . . I didn't recognise your voice on the telephone. I'm mad for you . . . Since the first moment I set eyes on you I've had nothing but the blues."

How many times had I closeted myself in the trunk of the Constellation of the Predecessors? Snugly cloistered, I would think about endless space, but as well of the echo of an atom of frost in the emptiness.

The porter's longing fed his confused excitation:

"All right . . . I'll be waiting at ten o'clock . . . in the Conservatory. . . . I won't say a word to my friend . . . to the caretaker. . . . He doesn't have to know, does he? . . . I love you so much, my darling. Come and we'll go away . . . forever. . . . Until tonight at ten—ten sharp!—my sweet torture!"

I watched myself, alone in the trunk. The trunk enclosed within the Firmament. The Firmament enclosed within the space of nothingness. There, inside, there subsisted neither idea nor absence of idea. The senses were stilled and so too was the understanding. Neither K—, nor the Maimed One, nor the Sisters, nor S—. . . . The spirit emptied itself out. I was present at the wedding of the infinite and the void.

Was S— aware of that immaterial, formless plane where our emotional and spatial categories did not apply?

"I have the conviction that the murderess is immaterial.

Pure sexuality. A sport of nature, in a way. A customer in the Bar told me—imagine the female Martian of your dreams."

Enclosed within the trunk I could make out an infinite range of worlds in an infinite space. And yet they all had the same structure, the same origin.

S—'s fascination went beyond the mere curiosity-seeker's interest.

"I have carried out a serious study. There have been no other murders with a straight razor, a barber's razor, anytime in the immediate past. The first was in the Cinema, the second that of the postman. . . . Surely the murderess is preparing a third. Perhaps she has wanted to kill since she became a woman."

S— was on the plane of desire and imagination and, occasionally, on the plane of dramatic expectation:

"I would like to meet her. Be her friend. Give her advice. Report her to the police. That is, report myself."

In the Firmament the waters of the Vat, the Electric Train, the fire on the Hearth, were time passing with no confusing images of remorsefulness, no labyrinths of glosses and explications. And without anyone else.

S— could hardly endure the *frisson* he felt before the facts on which the case was grounded:

"In the Bar the murderess asked for a cup of hot chocolate. At nine-thirty at night! It might have been the first time she had ever been in a bar. She sat at a table with a man old enough to be her grandfather. Serenely. The waiters pretended that she was a high-class whore. That is to say, she is a woman of some elegance and delicacy. Dressed, too, discreetly but elegantly . . . and, above all, not intimidated by being with a drunken old goat."

In the Firmament thought shaped itself into desires, pains, regrets, rationalizations, meditations. It was a spiritual *solfeggio extempore* which defied the lines and bars of real space.

S— delved into the romantic shades of *chiaroscuro:*

"Both times she has killed at night. She needs darkness. The light of day paralyses her. By day she would never take the razor out of her purse, not even under the most propitious conditions for murder. She is who she is beginning at nine or ten o'clock at night. I too am who I am only at night."

All things, without exception, even things incorporeal, were enclosed with me in the cabin trunk. Existence was as tiny as the flame of the tiny lamp. And yet, fed regularly with oil, it would never flicker out.

At the very verge of nothingness S— waited tirelessly, stuffed with sky and sheltered under that all-important, beloved exactitude of his:

"The murderess does not fear punishment, it doesn't frighten her that the police might arrest her. She no doubt doesn't believe in life. . . . So little in fact that she would not even commit suicide. She doesn't know that love exists."

Love was preserved in a grave in the ground of the greenhouse. It was constituted by a piece of chewed chewing gum I picked up in the street. It was so dry when I found it that it had the consistency of stone. When I would unbury it from time to time, I would contemplate the minute tracery of its wrinkles and creases. According to their alignment and position they might signify arms-waving or perhaps legs-trembling. On one occasion, I saw scratched on its surface the morning star.

For S— everything was portentous:

"The old man caressed her secretly and lasciviously in the Bar. Some say he touched her brazenly. Some say more discreetly. But everyone agrees that she neither discouraged nor incited him. Neither laughed nor showed outrage. She is an ascetic . . . like I am. She knows, as I do, that the nature of the flesh is unreal, gross, treacherous, and perverse. A customer told me, 'With what a fox like that drinks in a day, she wouldn't feel a thing, the old man's fingers wouldn't make a dent in her.' I believe it's that she sees her body as nothing more than a frying pan in the pantry. She doesn't see it, she doesn't feel it. And if someone touches it, she doesn't even notice."

Within the trunk I contemplated all of space in my cell. I felt as though I were walking a tightrope between infinity and the void. Between consciousness and unconsciousness. With one kick I could raise the lid and the trunk would cease to be Egg on the instant.

Did the caretaker establish the relationship and the path from one disequilibrium to another?:

"I knew you'd call me. . . . Ever since I left you I've been horny. I'm going up the walls. I wish I could get my hands on you right now. You've got me pussy-crazy. . . . And you're nothing but a world champion whore. But you're hot for me, aren't you?"

Everything was coördinated, one thing tied to another like concentric or dependent circles mysteriously obdurate.

The caretaker crowded stubbornly into the spotlight:

"At ten o'clock, in the Conservatory. That's a good time. I'm going to eat you alive. . . . But now that I think of it, my friend—the porter—he's going to be there. . . . Listen to what I tell you—I don't want you to so much as look at him. He's on this romantic kick these days. It's disgusting. If it goes any further he'll be writing you poetry. He hasn't realised what kind of woman you are, and that what you need isn't poetry but a good thick prick. I understand you, don't I, you pretty little bitch? You're like a steam boiler. You've got it so hot it sizzles."

What was love? What was the immediate splendour of the embrace of two arms?

The caretaker adorned himself in a pugnacious illusion:

"You know you bring out the beast in me. . . . I turn into a savage animal. And there's plenty of women after me. . . . But don't let the porter find out, he's pretty stiff-necked about things like that."

Sometimes, in the greenhouse, I would lie for hours with my eyes closed, in total darkness. When I opened them the Firmament would fill with light pouring in through the glass panes. The entire greenhouse, of a sudden, would be flooded with brilliance. Sunlight would illuminate the trunks, the flags and banners, the constellations, the monasteries of the Firmament. The earth would go to work. Centipedes would run along their old tracks. The buzzflies would come out of their hiding places and fly about, fluttering frenziedly as though in a hymn of adoration. The screwworms would squirm and crawl, writhe over all the level ground of the greenhouse. The water held in the Vat would be penetrated and transpierced by the rays of the sun. When I closed my eyes again the Firmament came to know night. Light and darkness were two twins with a common legacy. Like love and not-love? Like shrunken brightness and dilated shade?

The caretaker plunged into his own vortex:

"You left in such a hurry. You stood me up. Now I'm hornier than ever. You're mine. Your body belongs to me."

My body—was it the Firmament? The world? The cosmos? Space? A battlefield? A sacrificial victim provoking irresponsible executioners?

The caretaker tried to hide his terrible incertitude, the fact that he was adrift:

"I'll be waiting for you at ten sharp. In the Conservatory. And then we'll scram—we'll head for the cot!"

The Firmament, after the preservation of the cameo, brought forth a cosmovision project at once more modest and more ambitious than anything that had ever preceded it. More ambitious, in that thought was animated, so that I could be what I most truly was. And more modest in the sense that it recognised the impossibility of one's ever liberating oneself from the quotidian demands of life.

S— put a drop of perfumed oil on my right ear and a black female centaur in my hair. He looked at me as though he were gazing into a mirror.

"I'm so impatient! I don't know what I'll make of you, do with you. I might adorn your hair with water-roses and sprigs of cat-grapes. I could paint a tiny black vanessa antelope trimmed in yellow on your cheek. D— will be the master of ceremonies. I want him to know who you are."

When S— transformed me with his brushes, his make-up, his depilatories, his powders, his razors, I had the impression of seeing myself come alive. Would everything have been different had I been able to see myself slide into the light of day from the maternal womb? If I had witnessed the nine months of my gestation? I had the impression of having been born very, very late in relation to the day of my birth.

For S— the gloomy splendours were not conducive to concision:

"There will be people there from all over the world. The idle rich and the truly wealthy rich. D— has carefully chosen them. But it will be you who astonishes him, astounds him. I hope my uncle doesn't show up with that tacky male nurse of his."

Thoughts multiplied into infinitely meandering meditations. Implicitly, in the Firmament nothing was excluded. Neither unreality nor reality. Neither castles in the air nor melancholy. At one and the same time I might bring to my mouth the concentrated fires of a bonnet-pepper, of a bird pepper, and of the fierce *jalapeño* and swallow them like spoonfuls of water, like strands of insipid *chimeras.*

Anxiety was torturing S—:

"In the Castle, there will be no one like you."

Thought announced, it did not denounce. It was not the subject for predication, but rather the predicate, that which was predicated. The extremism fomented by ancient heterodoxies branched into so many tributaries that it finally dried up entirely. It was remembered as a positive element.

My spirit was accustomed to not withdrawing from physical reality. Thus the day might arrive when I would no longer know whether the spirit engendered the imperatives of reality or whether physical characteristics had been altered by the innovations of my spirit. The two things acted simultaneously.

How many hundred- or thousand-million species of insects had appeared and perished in the Firmament since the beginning of time? Who or what had determined that one species would perish and another survive, perdure?

Before I went to the Conservatory to tie the thread to the legs of the two hornets with my own hands, K— rehearsed the sacrifice for me.

WHY DID K— SHOW ME IN SUCH precise detail how he would bring about his own sacrifice? Did he plan to consummate it one day? When? What might motivate his suicide?

Dying, for K—: was it a solitary adventure or a public ceremony? He was willing to take his own life whenever he deemed it necessary. Did choosing between life and death seem to him absurd, frivolous, contemptible? Was courage for him living when one had to live and snuffing out life only when one had to die? Without degrees of existence? In the fulness of the instant?

"I am about to demonstrate immolation to you as though it were being portrayed on a stage, in a play. You will be able to follow all the steps of the offering. At the end of the ritual you will see how your participation will be essential if one day I have to cease to live."

K— was resting lightly on his knees on the floor, sitting back on his crossed feet. He opened the case. He took out two sabres swaddled in light grey linen.

The first funeral monument in the Firmament was a pyramid. I constructed it with mint candies all exactly the same size. With a knitting needle I introduced the drop of liquid into its central habitation, the first drop that issued from the womb-of-my-body. I deposited the drop in the brilliant green carapace of a scarab, on which I wrote, with great laboriousness, an epitaph. That was the first scarab with maxims in the greenhouse, the first message I hit upon. It came with the lapse from grace.

K— slipped one sabre from its sheath. Its almost blue steel gleamed like the blade of P—'s razor. He bound the blade with a wide ribbon of cloth. Only about twelve centimetres of the point of the sword were left free.

"Part of the blade of the sabre must be bound so that it can be manipulated without cutting the hands. The handle will not be within reach during the sacrifice."

Life for K— was a precious gift of nature. He believed that it should not be uselessly placed in danger. What disorder might shatter the harmony of life and the universe, such that one might sacrifice existence in an act of suicide?

The mint-candy pyramid was surprisingly large. It was the largest funerary monument in the Firmament, and yet its sole mission and purpose was to preserve one drop of my blood.

K— unsheathed the other sabre. He placed it on the carpet, behind him.

"This is the sword the assistant will use. That is, the sword you will wield when the ritual is done. The sabre, as you see, is not a scimitar, but it does have a long thick handle which allows you to hold it with both hands."

Death and sex—were they, for K—, two unforeseeable and powerfully malignant manifestations of nature? Did he wish to control these two blinding eruptions? When K— practised *sumo* he managed to raise his testicles into the cavity of his body. The fire of his faith—did it keep watch over the fatality of his *naïveté?*

In the Firmament, funeral rites were very much the same as cultural celebrations. Every day I would bury one of the insects which morning had found dead. I would blow into its mouth and its eyes. So it would be reborn into another life? Into another Firmament outside this world? As I wrapped the remains of the insect in strips of cigarette paper I pretended to cry and whimper softly. For insects, was dying sleeping? In a garden of flowers? So that it might be nourished in what was known as the Sleep of Death I placed certain nutriments beside the deceased—a crumb of bread and a speck of sugar. At the gate of the Catacomb of the Mummies where I buried them I had set a cast-lead grasshopper painted red. With its forelegs raised in an attitude of aggressive defence, would it assure that the catacomb would be protected until the day of the insects' resurrection? Did the insects believe in a great beyond, as the Maimed One did? Even though that locked them into the humiliating servitude of constantly inventing and reinventing an era of love under the guise of eternity?

K— opened his tunic, and his naked body, centred on his cosmic belly, appeared.

"One wears a wide sash of white linen, as you see, pushed far down below the navel. He who would take his own life leaves thus exposed his most spiritual part."

K— closed his eyes. With three fingers of his left hand he slowly massaged his abdomen.

"Ideally one commits suicide under the cherry blossoms, which are the symbol of the beautiful—and the ephemeral."

He continued massaging his belly. With this ceremony would K— master death? Or would its blind violence destroy him? Would his pure, clean generosity crumble the impetuous caprices of the universe?

"The hero concentrates on the solemn act he is about to perform. He touches his belly to be certain that it will be offered in a state of complete relaxation. The point of entry for the sword cannot display even the least sign of twitching. Slowness, decision, serenity."

At the gate of the Catacomb of the Mummies, beside the lead grasshopper, I planted a pencil, point downwards. It was the key to the Book of the Dead. The book was a tiny cardboard box. On rocks and stones and steles I engraved the names of the first mummified insects.

Shifting his weight to his knees, K— lightly sat more erect. He picked up the sabre. He raised it like a trophy, and then, with his right hand, he grasped it at the linen binding. With both hands, he turned the sabre towards himself. He bent very slightly toward the point of the blade aimed at his belly.

"The steel must enter here. To the left of the navel and below it. About ten centimetres. At the centre of equilibrium."

K— showed with the sharp point of the sword a location in his entrails. Did he bring such order to death so as to suppress its chaos? To rob it of its suddenness, its brusqueness? To bring a halt to the celebrated risks of a proudly lived existence?

Were insects able without confusion to resort to magic? Did they have at their disposal maps with which to cross the regions of the beyond? Did they have formulas and prescriptions for dealing with those regions without danger? Did Purgatory exist for them, as it did for the Sisters and the Maimed One? Did Limbo? The prayers and supplications which one supposed them to recite—were they threats? Could an ant-lion be reborn as a crab-louse? As a tse-tse fly? As a liver fluke? A leech? A malarial mosquito? A tapeworm? A prometheus moth?

According to legend, the ants of the Firmament in their dying moments recited, like litanies, declarations of innocence directed to the Sun:

"I present myself to thee who art about to judge me—

"I have committed no iniquity whatever against worker or warrior.

"I have enslaved no ant from another nest nor any inferior insect.

"I have committed no abomination against thee who art justice.

"I have not caused anyone to die of hunger, and my granaries and storehouses have been open even to the horned scarab.

"I have made no one cry, least of all the queen ant.

"I have not killed or ordered killing.

"I have not cheated thee who art justice of thy gifts and offerings.

"I have been pure, six times pure as the number of my legs.

"My purity has been that of The Egg over Phat."

For the ants, Phat was the temple of opulence. It stood in the centre of the dungheap.

Did K— identify himself with that bold and reckless trance?

"The hero sustains the sabre. One powerful impulse and the steel slashes into his belly. A cut ten centimetres deep is made in his body at that instant. For several seconds the sword plunged into his entrails remains immobile. The pain is so intense that he thinks the heavens have crushed him. It is a torment so unexpected, in spite of the fact that he has meditated over this act for years, that the self-sacrificer has a sensation of chaos. In spite of the efforts he makes to control his breathing, he breathes with great difficulty. A fiery agony consumes him, gnaws away at his brain. All his resolve, all his courage, all his will are threatened. He fears above all that he will tremble."

With the point of the sabre, with a quick-breathed pulse of his naked belly, K— demonstrated the sacrifice. He spoke without moving his head, without lowering his gaze to his navel. He was living the *simulacrum:*

"He feels the blood trickle down his abdomen, his groin, his thighs, to his knees. The immense pain does not cease. In fact it continually grows, but he knows that the sacrifice has only just begun."

The insects of the Firmament, the invaders, the first settlers to inhabit the greenhouse, the immigrants and the *conquistadores*—did they have some concept of the Firmament directly related to funeral rites? Why did they preserve their bodies after death in a special area of their nests? The long chain of insect dynasties succeeded one another without changing these customs. How did they interpret the Catacomb of the Mummies that I had constructed? In their rites, why did they so carefully and precisely distinguish between the ceremony of dying, death itself, and the burial, the different shapes of fatality and of initiative, free will?

K— was perspiring though he was very pale:

"After the brief pause with the sword lodged in his viscera, the hero needs both his hands. He firmly, steadfastly holds the sabre still. He begins to cut his belly from left to right, parallel to the ground. The blade encounters the obstacle of his intestines. Their elasticity makes the incision difficult. He must bear down with both hands and with all his strength. He crosses the navel and continues ten centimetres more to the right. Thus concludes the first stage of the sacrifice."

The first funerary monument, the pyramid, was built of mint candies because of the structural solidity of that material. It was by definition the stuff of eternity. The chamber in which the drop of my blood was housed in its bed of chitinous carapace evoked darkness/light. Could the hierarchies darkness/light, evil/good, night/day, be justified? Had categories, as a far-off schism wanted to do, been established? Categories of diverse groups, objects, trunks, flags and banners, animals, paintings? Categories of diverse cults? Categories of what K— called "the gods"? The window-panes were situated above the sand of the greenhouse, the Vigorous Mountains above the Vat. But everything beneath was like what was above. Therefore the structural substance of a water-strider's legs or a chip from the nave of a temple was the exact reflexion of the most intimate structure of primordial stuff, its outward and visible sign and silent immanent secret.

For K—, would suddenly dying have been a curse, have been damnation? Would it have been the abominable, monstrous act *par excellence*?

"The intestines emerge from his open belly. The hero's mouth wants to scream, yet his spirit remains serene. The great rent in his abdomen vomits blood and intestines."

K—, acting out his suicide, raised the sword with his right hand. With feigned difficulty:

"The upraised sword reeches with filth, with blood, with greasy exudation. But the hero has managed to heave the weapon up. He must be firm with himself lest his hand tremble. All about him there is a pool of blood. His head droops."

The Firmament, just as it was, just as it looked— did the Marvellous shine through it from beneath? Was it almost vaporously fragile? When, before I slept, I sprawled on the rush mat and contemplated the constellations, the monasteries, the paths, the temples, the systems I had so laboured to construct, I feared that everything might be crumbled and destroyed, razed, suddenly, like a sand castle by a sudden wave. Why did everything remain standing? Some internal dynamism kept the greenhouse alive: In the Firmament, was there an opposition between Essence and Existence, between Energy and Necessity, between transcendent energy and blind necessity? Was there an opposition between the brutal fire of invading unity and the pullulations in darkness of that which was hidden? All living creatures in the greenhouse used the liberty lent by the greenhouse as a gift they received by virtue of their mere existence in it. This spiritual state of affairs entailed practical consequences at all levels, even at the level of behaviour. The tiny minnows of the Vat, according to this principle of analogy, were true reflexions of the image of the Firmament. They were in their turn emanation and manifestation of its energy. From this perspective nothing was trivial, insignificant, futile, puerile. It was remembered that in the past there had been a celebration of the day a fleck of plaster fell from the wall of the greenhouse. One sect of the origins maintained the idea that if even the most minute and apparently insignificant act were not carried out perfectly, the sun would not appear in the mornings through the great glass panes of the greenhouse. It was a period known as Theological Delirium.

Did K— imagine a time intermediate between death and the definitive end of existence? With his fallen head resting on his left clavicle and his right hand holding the sword aloft, K— sat motionless for a few seconds. His half-closed eyes seemed to look at the pool of blood which only existed in his imagination:

"The hero's work is done. The sacrifice must now be

concluded. One minute later he can be aided by his assistant."

K— took the second sabre and stood up. He asked me to stand directly beside him.

"Observe carefully. When the pain has reached its zenith the assistant kills the hero with the second blade. He is decapitated so that his suffering can come to an end and the sacrifice be culminated."

With both hands K— raised the sabre above his right shoulder. He cleft the air with one great stroke, as though acting out his own decapitation.

In the Firmament, I would ask myself, "Will all this be consumed one day? At the end of what term of eternity? Will all be dust one day? Hermetic particles of ash sunk into invariability? At what moment will there no longer be any distinction between the rusted shell of a steel ball bearing and the cadaver of a green caterpillar?"

W HEN I ARRIVED AT THE CONSERV-
atory it was ten o'clock at night. In my bag I was
carrying the straight razor that had been P—'s gift to me.

The caretaker and the porter had readied themselves for the
Soirée. Each in his own way wanted the forces of darkness, the
power of destruction, to triumph. It frightened them to be
two. A competitive tension was immediately created between
them.

What was aggression? How would it be expressed? What
consequences did it have? What negative effects on group
survival did it entail? The warrior-ants of the greenhouse
would attack their opposite numbers with their mandibles like
wire-cutters, like strong pliers. Blinded by the fury of their
own aggressiveness? Could they possibly have renounced it?
Did they, in exchange for the opportunity to attack their com-
petitors, resign themselves to the possibility that their own
species might be extinguished? What satisfaction did they experience when at the end of the battle they contemplated the
field strewn with pieces of thoraces and abdomens, amputated
legs, and broken and truncated antennae?

Both wore clean shirts. The caretaker's was completely un-
buttoned. The porter displayed a necktie tight around his
neck. The caretaker knew nothing of the methods for reaching
spiritual fulfilment. He was narrowly enclosed within his own
body.

"But . . . what the . . . ? Did he know you were coming to
see me tonight?"

Certain pupiparous flies could, like the caretaker, go through periods of intense agitation. Did they wish to discover the limits of their physical, sexual energies? Did the disorder of their impulses engender ambivalent consequences? Did they seize upon these passionate energies in order to transform them into acts?

"I had no idea that you and my friend had made an . . . appointment . . . for the same time and place as you and . . . I . . . had. Do you mean it never occurred to you that you had already made plans?"

"Hey, why don't you just please go? She and I have a lot of things to discuss here."

"I'm the one that has to talk to her . . . and about important things . . . things that concern you . . ."

Was there a model for aggressive behaviour? Was it acquired partially by learning? Or completely? Was it imparted at birth, by simply being born? Was the affliction shared by all?

Who would write the last page of the porter's and the caretaker's lives? When I wrote out the biography of the first minnow attacked and disembowelled in the Vat by another individual of its species, I attempted to prevent the paraphrase from replacing the phenomenon. At that time the Vat was known as the Lake of *Lepisma saccharina*. About that time I constructed a dam which disintegrated when I filled it with water. Because I had not given it a name? Until a thing was named was it not possessed? From that day on the ruins presided over the Plain of Mercy. A legend transmuted the facts: it recounted that when I raised a wall by day, by night, as I slept, it was destroyed of its own accord. Did this suggest a symbol of the effects of aggressive behaviour? Was violence a floating energy, always available and at hand?

"No way you're staying here in the library in the middle of the Conservatory, at ten o'clock at night, with two guys— alone. What kind of idea is that? You want us to get into a cockfight over you, huh? Is that it? Well, you're very bloody goddamn mixed up, then. I'm going to take you and have a

few words with you—alone—to help out what's-his-name
there."

"I was counting on this. You've no idea how I'd dreamed
. . . See the tie I put on for you? . . . my wedding tie . . . All
right, I'm married. . . . But you already knew that, didn't you?
. . . But it's all so different with you!"

"Cut the romantic crap. You're acting sillier than a stuffed
penguin. The best thing you could do for yourself is take off.
I'm the one she made the first date with."

"*You* leave, once and for all. I'm the one who loves her. I'm
in love with her. Do you hear me? . . . So why don't you leave
us two alone—what's it to you? You hate her anyway."

"Sure I hate her. I hate her guts. Because she's a dirty little
whore that's sucking your soul out like a vampire. I'm not
going to stand by and let her get away with it. . . . I'm doing
this for your own good. You're blind, you're obsessed with
her, and you can't even see it. Listen, the little conversation
I'm going to have with her . . . it's about you. . . . I don't think
you ought to be listening. . . . When I straighten this out I'll
tell you all about it, I'll give you a blow-by-blow description.
So go on, get going."

Under what conditions, what tensions, did aggressiveness
arise? Was it an imbalance constantly latent which would burst
forth under abnormal circumstances? Did insects think the
Electric Train was a god of war to whom individuals of their
species had to be sacrificed? The Train, twice each day, made
a circuit of the greenhouse along its border with the outside
walls. The powerful locomotive light was always burning. It
would return to me with its forward wheels and face bloody,
covered with the squashed, splattered remains of insects. Did
the huge, hurtling light of the locomotive frighten the insects?
Did they imagine that it was some bark from Hell? Did they
assume that it achieved such velocity because it created a void
in front of itself? Whom did they sacrifice? Which of their
fellows were transformed into a quick burst of scintillation
ground to dust by destiny?

Head-hunting, cannibalism, physical mutilations, scalping,

wars of extermination, human sacrifice—did these arise as complex responses to inexplicable tensions, docile vocations inflamed by the call of the flesh?

The caretaker and the porter veiled their amazement with prophecies:

"Well, now, sweetheart, what is it you've come to us looking for? Such sweet memories of the basement the other night, right? You shit!"

"Don't treat her like that. Stop insulting her. You hurt *me* when you hurt her. It feels like you were stabbing me."

"What! You poor innocent baby! Can't you see she's a whore! With the face of an angel, sure, a good little girl . . . but I'd bet my life she's older than she looks . . . a lot older. If you ask me she's made a pact with the devil like I saw one time in the movies. . . . This guy looked practically like a kid . . . but a picture of him got older and older. I'll tell you, you ever see this baby's picture, you'll fall right back out of love so fast . . ."

"If all you're going to do is insult her, why don't you leave and let us be together?"

"You can't be in love with a tramp, a little pigeon like this. I'm here to put an end to all that. Like it or not. You mean you still haven't realised that this little bitch will do anything, and I mean *anything,* with anybody? You mean you've forgotten how she turned us both on the other night? Every time we'd had enough she'd get it up for us again. You don't remember that? That way she looks at you? . . . Look, all I've gotta do is think about it again . . . I get furious. . . . If I didn't control myself, I'd beat her to a pulp."

"What good would that do? . . . Calm down, now."

At the Roof of the Firmament there rose a region as violent, as tumultuous, as its tracks, its trails, its crags, its mountain passes, its cliffs, its precipices, its chasms and abysses, its peaks which almost touched the glass panes of the sky. The insects which chose those haunts were impatient and brusque, empirical, and eager for tangible results. Did they adore the bolt of lightning which destroyed them . . . and illuminated them?

According to the caretaker, the porter should not squander his forces. He might lose himself down dusty byways. Or drown:

"You're going to be the one to lose. Think of your wife. Your kids. Think of yourself. Your own life. You can't just toss all that out the window for some nickel-and-dime one-night stand. I don't see how you can lose your head over some bitch who'll have you walking the dogs down Bitter Street in two days."

"Stop worrying about me. I'm old enough to know what I'm doing. I've said it once and I'll say it again—as politely as I know how—why don't you butt out once and for fucking all."

"Right, so you can roll around all over the floor with her."

"Just leave us be, will you?"

"How could you ever think I'd leave you be, buddy? I'm here to help you."

"If you really want to help me, you'll beat it."

"I'm going to help you against yourself, you stubborn shit."

"I don't need anything from you."

"I'm not letting you kill yourself."

When I looked at the caretaker's eyes, the furrowed wrinkles of his forehead, the shape of his ears . . . I realised that these isolated images were fleeting visions which could not explain an individual's totality. In the portraits of the Maimed One the features in repose, painted for all eternity, were motionless labyrinths. The eyes in the paintings had a certain indefinite piercing quality. Were they the concentrically circular symbols of the infinity of the spirit? Places of secrets, realms of surprises, indiscreet revelations brought back up from deep-descending, invading roots? When I buried my hands for a few moments in the soil of the greenhouse, I felt firm and unyielding, impassive. When the breeze turned the windmill on the Field of the Law, did it set in motion the doctrines of the Firmament?

"You see what she's doing! She's taking off her clothes! I told you what kind of so-called girl this was! . . . Oh . . . look at her! Holy shit! . . . And she likes it!"

"You're going to scare her, yelling like that. . . . Look what you've made her do."

"Nobody told anybody to get naked."

"Yes, but last time you . . . playing the stud . . ."

"Not that you didn't eat out of the same trough, my friend, or don't you remember?"

"Don't look at her like that, you've got no right."

"That's the last straw. . . . Listen, I'm a man and I've got the equipment to prove it. . . . And if she cranks up my engine . . . I mean the bitch is standing there stark staring naked!"

"How can you be so vulgar to her?"

"I'll treat her any way I want to . . . right, you sweet bitch?"

What labyrinth of spiritual permutations was produced by aggression? How many millions of billions of neurons in the human brain had been required to give birth to competitive behaviour? Did aggression drown muscular, sensory, glandular, spiritual differences between people? Did the owl moth and the longicorn beetle, at birth, feel lost in a maze of infinite complication? How were they guided so as to learn and to choose? Effectiveness and quickness—did that lead them inexorably to aggressiveness, fanning its embers, exciting their flames of desire?

"You've got that look in your eye when you look at her. That dirty look. You make me sick!"

"How do you think you're looking at her?"

"Get out. . . . I'm staying here with her . . . all by ourselves . . . just the two of us . . . but we won't do anything. . . . You don't know what it means to love a woman."

"I don't want to know, either."

"Get out of here, right now. Can't you see she can't stand you?"

"That just shows how much you know about little whores like this one. . . . You want me to tell you why she's stripped naked like that, just because she felt like it, without anybody asking her to? Because she remembers what we gave her in the basement. She's just dreaming about doing that number again. See, once you get a taste of it . . . Two pieces of meat at the same time is a real feast! You don't know women. It's the way you move, when you . . . move . . . right? right? . . . that drives them crazy. They'll do anything! I'm telling you, I know what I'm talking about."

"I forbid you to touch her."

"She's *begging* for it. You poor bastard."

The caretaker picked my underpants up off the floor. What spiritual trajectory had aggression followed? The simian being that lived in trees four million years ago, the individual who fifty thousand years ago began to use the first real language, and the man who, at last, believed that the interpretation of the truth was independent of his way of conceiving the functioning of the spirit—could they feel aggression evolving like will, like the size of hands, like intelligence or the way of walking, like a mute creation which conferred its inexhaustible wisdom and its blood-curdling doom on them?

"Smell these panties! You could eat them stewed in their own juices."

"Stop that . . . they're hers."

The caretaker chewed my underwear. With his hands and teeth he ripped and tore them.

"Look what you're doing! That's enough!"

"I should have ripped them with the end of my prick. That's what she was waiting for."

"Why do you have to take advantage of the situation? If I could . . . I'd brain you."

The caretaker finally ripped my underwear to shreds with his teeth. Then he picked up my bag and opened it. In a sort of fury he turned it upside down, and its contents spilled out onto the floor. P—'s razor first. One of the maxims, written on a cigarette paper, fluttered to the ground.

The butterfly and the longicorn beetle—what laws guided them the first time they behaved aggressively? In order to begin, what specific rules, what principles of causality must they have innately possessed? What burning orders and directives, what necessities dawned as they escaped from their larval past?

"All you have is brute force, and you use it to bring her to her knees, to humiliate her."

"Hey—what's this? . . . A barber's razor. See how strange this little pigeon of yours is—god knows what she was planning to do with this cavalry sword."

"Let her have whatever she wants to. How would *you* like it if somebody went through your pockets."

"Shit! What an edge on it!"

The caretaker pulled out a hair and split it. Then he put the razor down on a table covered with magazines.

"Who'd you steal the razor from? One of the guys you sleep with? What about me? What're you going to steal from me? I'll have to wait and see. . . . Come here! . . . On your knees. . . . That's it! . . . Now start sucking, bitch! . . . Oh, you're so good! . . . Who taught you to suck a prick like that?"

The porter staggered backwards, livid, dumbstruck, open-mouthed in dismay. Was he seeing without seeing? Was he crestfallen? Driven out of his wits? Furious? Spellbound?

Were there universal rules of conduct across diverse species? Was there an instinct of aggression common to all? What charge of aggressiveness could any individual bear? Had debilitating forms of aggressiveness ever appeared? Protective? Destructive? Could one prove interactions between aggressiveness and the diminution of mobility in the motor systems? Did aggressiveness stimulate tensions? Destabilize the physiology? Create situations of cerebral emergency? Enslave the functioning of the blood? Were the most harmful secondary effects of aggression still unknown? Did it support deeds of adventure gropingly performed in the maw of dusky darkness and transition?

The porter staggered even further backward. Did he want the earth to swallow him? To encrust himself into the wall?

"No . . . no . . . no . . ."

"No? Why not? . . . You see how she gobbles it down.

. . . You poke it to her from the back . . . like in the basement. See, business is picking up. 'Course, you can't get into her on your knees. . . . She's asking for it with her eyes."

Behind the caretaker, the porter was watching us in horror.

In the Firmament any evil or good act performed with full knowledge automatically and inexorably redounded to its author. Positive or negative retribution, the oscillation of doubt between the temblors of absolute enigma.

Behind the caretaker, the porter picked up the razor and began to step forward. The two hornet's legs were now firmly tied together.

"That's it, come on! Closer! Touch her. She'll show you how much she appreciates it, I guarantee. You don't even have to let your pants down. Ram it in till it comes out her throat! Come on!"

The porter, with P—'s razor, slashed the caretaker's back. Just at the level of his heart. And then immediately he slashed him again just under his right ear.

K— HANDED ME A LETTER TIED IN A saffron-yellow ribbon. He asked me to read it later that night. Before I went to sleep.

Impatience—did it, as one schism affirmed, estrange us from life? It had been said that impatience might lodge in one of three residences—the Colourless Palace of the Brain, the Red Castle of the Heart, or the Sulphur Mine just below the Navel. Where was S—'s?

"I'm dying of impatience. I've bought the tickets—we'll go to the Castle by train. How long we have to wait!"

The cuckoo-fly's agitation, its disorderly and excited behaviour—what did it mean? There were moments in the Firmament when evidence was to be had that time did not pass so fast as it seemed to, but rather that *we* did. When I fleetingly glimpsed the locomotive of the Electric Train flying at top speed past the abyss of the Crags of Dogma—were the moment and Eternity made one? Did time flee at the speed of the locomotive? Did endurance, which it stubbornly pursued, endlessly elude it? Retreat to the immutable suspendedness of oblivion?

Everything pointed to S— as a centre of nonsense and vacuity:

"What do you think—I could dress you in tulle? But I like you in the evening gown, too, the one cut all the way down in back, with the ruffles. Oh, and you should wear lilac-coloured underwear, trimmed in black lace. . . . I can't make up my mind. I'm like an impatient bride."

The elder Sister would give the Maimed One a long facial massage before combing his hair. Lying back, almost spread-eagled in a great chair with the back tilted as far as it could be, the Maimed One, with his eyes closed, would complain:

"They say that we are living through a crisis, yet in reality we are passing through the worst imaginable decadence. When He dies, the little that remains to us of decisiveness and will will be drowned. Under the spotlights of television crews, emboldened by every revenge-seeker on the planet, the slug-gards and the begrudging of the earth will overrun the Keep."

The younger Sister, meanwhile, with a basin for his fingers on her lap, painstakingly manicured the Maimed One's hands. On the moveable table beside her were arranged scissors, files, cuticle clippers, an orange stick, a flask of lavender-water, toothpaste, a glass, two toothbrushes, two towels, cotton, swabs, a sleeve-protector. The Maimed One feared the irre-sistible and utterly certain hell to follow:

"We will escape in my old auto. They will not stop us. We live in the very centre of the zone of most active turbulence. Our lives will be in danger."

When the younger Sister finished her exertions over the Maimed One's fingers, she brushed his teeth. She did it in such a way that he did not have to move his head from the cushion on the chair-back, and without disturbing the massage her sister was at the same time performing on him.

"The Keep has been readied for the assault. You have put the principal things into boxes, luggage, steamer trunks . . . although there are still things either to be sent to the green-house or to be thrown into the fire. Civilisations die, just as we do, after the long agony of decadence."

The three people immersed themselves in the most cow-ardly imaginable dance: in this last epoch, they had created a nomadic civilisation within the Keep. Its centre of gravity shifted according to historical circumstances: the bedroom, the hall, the kitchen, the music room, the dining room, the library, each saw its respective, and fugitive, era of prosperity. The television room at last became the nucleus of the house's only activity. The Maimed One, in a symbiosis with the room from which he no longer stirred, spent his days in pyjamas and a dressing gown, his one foot shod in an embroidered slipper with a tassel.

When S— spoke of the Soirées he grew extremely heated:

"There have been two more murders. This time at the Conservatory. Two cadavers with their throats cut have been found in the library. Signed by the same murderess—with her straight razor. At least that is the police version. And it is true that the conditions call to mind the previous murders. I very tenuously begin to feel what the murderess feels before the love/death duality."

The invisible pairs grace/power, feeling/action, melancholy/hopefulness, like the nooks and crannies and changing moods of the Firmament, lent variety to the Firmament's perspectives.

"Now that the police force has been hypnotised by the double assassination in the Conservatory, I have carried out further investigations on the letter carrier. In tranquillity. I found his former lover. She is a very decided young lady. She told me that the postman was in love with her obsessively. According to her, he went through deliriums of interpretation. He would write her several letters a day. They lived together for several months in his apartment. After their parting he would wait for her every night at the bus stop in front of her office. Therefore, on the evening he was murdered he watched from a distance as his former lover, as always, got on her bus, and then he turned to walk through the Park to his home. All the police know is that he was found with his throat slashed in his apartment, after having had an orgasm. I can imagine him, at nine o'clock when his old flame had left her office, walking in agitation and turmoil, in a daze of his obsession, through the trees and clumps of foliage. He was a queerly particular, meticulous person, even in the way he loved. His lover was bored by his collection of lead soldiers and his invariably selfsame kisses. She could not stand the victrola which inevitably started up each time they opened the door of his habitation. His initiative had shrivelled to zero. All was routine. So far as she was concerned, he behaved like a broken record. This is the man the murderess bumped into in the Park."

What was love? Was it an allegory of the hour of death? Did a couple perform for it the dance of the loins, in the centre of creation? What was pleasure? Could it be known? Felt? Was it the sooty smoke and fumes from lumpish hopes?

"The murderess and the postman stand out as two utterly opposed, mismatched beings. It is remarkable that they would ever have met. What was she doing at night in the Park? Had she arranged to meet him there? It may be worthwhile to ask where they could previously have met. My own hypothesis is that the murderess had arranged to meet some third person, who never came. Perhaps a foreigner who had been misunderstood because of some difficulty with the language. Perhaps he had mentioned eight-thirty in the morning and she had thought he was referring to eight-thirty at night. A woman like she is might wait for hours with no impatience, no irritation, without being in the least perturbed. She is perfectly capable of lying down peacefully on a bench and contemplating the starry night . . . or even of going to sleep and dreaming."

Among the moths of the greenhouse pleasure predominated. Among the termites, procreation. Pleasure and procreation—were they the two terrible, sombre forces at work in the Firmament? Traitors to glory? Were they the instinctive dross of a lost paradise?

"The postman, upset and deeply moved, once more, by the nostalgia awakened in him by the vision of his former mistress, walks through the hedges of *arborvitae*. He has just watched her step up onto the bus and ride away. It is a dark night, but suddenly he seems to see a shape on a stone bench there in the Park. A feminine body. From a distance, how much it resembles his beloved's! He approaches . . . to caress her . . . to beg her to come back to him. I can almost see him, when his hand touches the side, or the heart, of the murderess . . . and she wakes up. How disappointing!"

What was the relation between the idea of love and the visual image of the beloved? Love and odour—did they set in motion the same spiritual machinery? The green caterpillar—when it slithered up the stalk—could it, thanks to odour, imagine the flower it could not yet see? What must the photograph have been like which was printed on its cerebral molecules—the print of the concept Flower?

"His mistress, his beloved, has just told me how the postman performed the act of sex. Apparently her role in the service was virtually passive. In the ceremony only her hands and her mouth took part. To the point that even today she asks herself whether her womb inspired some repugnance in him. There is no doubt whatever that he loved her, I would even go so far as to say with insane devotion. And yet, let me point out, he had her get on her knees. Practically to worship him. While he, belly up as it were, covered his face with a pillow, as though he didn't want to see her, as though he wished to be alone with only the image of her. I am convinced that he demanded that the murderess play the role of his beloved. Perhaps even to the point of having her dress in one of the dresses which he still kept. At any rate, to the point of having her repeat, meticulously and minutely, each and every one of her movements and gestures. So that when the murderess, with one stroke, cut his throat, the postman was closer than he had ever been in his life if not to happiness then to pleasure. Perhaps he was seeing, projected onto his brain, the thousand photographs he had taken of his naked mistress."

Had photography, like figurative art of forty thousand years ago, arisen to serve as an archive? To register the stature and position of each individual in relation to another or to the collective? Was the number of photographic or carven representations of a single person important? Did it make a difference? Have some significance? Beginning at which image, what number, would a qualitative change in the hierarchy of flowers long ago cut be effected?

S— still worried his bone:

"The newspapers talk about the two Conservatory em-

ployees as though they were two fingers of one same hand.
They both died the same night, it is true, but in very different
ways. How can the authorities not have noticed? The caretaker is the sensual male incarnate, lascivious, a man whose
appetites were voracious. The other man, the porter, is the
epitome of the good married man, fragile, bashful, mediocre,
yet sensitive and given to falling in love. The night of the
murder he probably showed himself to be as timid as the
caretaker reveals himself to be forthright and quick to act. But
why are we given to understand, as a certainty, that the two
men were both killed by the murderess? There is no doubt
that the murderess slit the porter's throat. The murder was
carried out in the same way as the first two times. But the
caretaker was not murdered like the others. He was the victim
of two clumsy cuts—one at his back and the other just here,
under his right ear. Two strokes as though befuddled and yet
violent, so unlike the murderess's serenity. I believe the
mouselike porter killed his friend. Perhaps when he saw that
he was his rival. Perhaps out of fear."

What influence did fear have over the formation of intelligence? Did the first intelligent acts consist of remembering
some terrors or intimidations, refeeling those emotions at a
considerable distance of time? Were fear and intelligence directly associated? Had fear produced the first intelligent laws,
thanks to which the first dangers, some two million years ago,
could be confronted? Did the scheme of decisions and innovations inspired by fear give impetus to the development of
intelligence? But this first intelligence—did it not have as a
consequence the increase of alertness or attention, and, therefore, of fear? And this ever-growing fear—did it in turn fo-
ment a more and more complex intelligence? Like a thick
thread basting patches of thought together in the quilt of
consciousness?

"What is indisputable is that the murderess already knew
the caretaker and the porter when she appeared that night in
the Conservatory. Given their psychological differences, one
might easily suppose that the porter had fallen in love with the

murderess and that the caretaker was frothing like a dog in heat to bed her. She arranges to meet both the men at the same time, the rutting stallion and the pining prince, the loins and the heart, and she sets them face to face. All my life I have dreamt of seeing such a wonderful battle."

K— would narrate the legend of the first duel: the first man who surprised his brother making love to his wife established the rules of the first duel. The husband, with a club, was allowed to strike the lover's head as hard as he could. Then the lover could deal the husband one blow. The rivals, now bloodied but without losing their dignity when it was their turn to be the victim, would alternately club each other until one of the two fell dead. And so they did it.

How could individuals divest themselves of their ancestral choices? By sheer caprice? From what moment onward would they mate with members of the group not of their own family? From what moment onward would they cease scrabbling in their own dungheaps? Why did the majority esteem the Sweet, like the pollinator-wasp?

"I have the impression that the police have fewer clews than I do . . . and some of them are false. Apparently they have conceived the idea of setting bait out for the murderess. I believe that will prove a misguided strategy . . . and as though not misguided enough, a newspaper has printed a report on it. They are preparing a composite portrait! It will be utterly useless! I have spoken to all the witnesses in the Bar. Some say she is brunette, some say she is blond . . . or even has chestnut-coloured hair! They cannot agree whether she is tall or short, or has blue eyes or green. So I ask you—in the absence of any concrete features, can they possibly produce a composite picture?"

In the Firmament when I thought I had explained some intellectual phenomenon I always realised that, when all was said and done, it still kept its secret, as though its pulse throbbed endlessly.

I collapsed onto the *tatami* mat with the letter K— had given me. Each constellation, each planet, every grain of sand, every molecule of dust, each drop of water, each atom, each proton, every miasmic breath, every electron acted of its own accord as though it were related only to itself. And yet the Firmament preserved its coherence, its order, its structure. Everything knew everything . . . about nothing?

I opened the envelope and read K—'s message:

"This morning in the Park a heather-flower blossomed. I contemplated it. I immersed myself in it. I forgot myself. I sat and stared at it for hours. I entered it. What a lovely breeze! What delightful petals! What joy! What a perfect life—and so short! May you always be like that flower!"

D ID K— WANT ME TO ACCOMPANY
him?:

"When I end my cycle in your country I will return on foot
to my own, that of my ancestors. I will cross more than half
a world, like a wandering hermit. I will spend years walking.
At the various stages I will communicate with people by way
of pictorial expressions of spirituality. I will project the breath
of knowledge onto an aesthetic plane."

Was painting, to K—'s mind, a kind of glossolalia? The
tongues of fire to which S— referred? Did he feel mistrust for
language, or fervour?

"All along the road I will trace the Way."

To what "Way" did K— allude? Those pictorial images—
were they visions or mere glimpses? These images—would
they portray the shell of the spirit? Reflect its essence? Its
naked transparency and its penitential delirium?

For K— a voyage was the equivalent of an itinerary of
transformation. In the greenhouse, insects evolved in quite
distinct stages. The life of the ephemerid, the mayfly, never
lasted more than a few hours though they might remain larvae
for more than three years. The flying stag beetle, when it
emerged from its chrysalis at the end of summer, did not crawl
toward the surface but rather lay immobile, buried, for close
onto a year, hidden beneath Carpenters' Field. Black flies, if
their eggs had been laid in the Quadrangle of Unspeakable
Filth, required fewer than ten days to pass through the entire
cycle of egg-larva-pupa-adult.

S— dreamt of the trip to the Castle:

"I have received word that guests are beginning to arrive at the Castle. D— sent a telegram to my uncle. It said:

> Apotheosis, licence, fascination. The most depraved couples in the world are on their way to the Castle in aircraft loaded with cauliflower, tacks, and *prie-dieux*. I will only admit sublime sadomasochists or frenzied paranoids. It will be the most maddeningly delicious and edible evening of the century in the most irrational and mystical nation of the universe. I send you my most supergelatinous and putrescent devotion.
>
> Divinely yours . . .

"What I would like, if I could have any wish I made, would be to go to the Castle with two women—you as my mistress and the murderess as my slave."

S— dreamt of being carried away to the summit of consciousness, but K— meditated over his itinerary:

"My ancestors thought that a goddess gave birth to every thing which exists. From her womb sprang islands, seas, mountains, rivers, metals, rocks, plants, and trees."

The day my loins lost my first drop of blood the genesis of the Firmament was begun. I was at that time thirteen years old. K— arrived two years afterward.

"The goddess gave birth last of all to fire. This birth left her with burns on her loins. The pain brought on vomiting and horrible sweat. Her excrement, her urine, her pus, her sweat, her vomit were transformed into creatures and nine gods."

A few days after losing my first drop of blood, I removed the hymen-of-my-body with the hands-of-my-thorax and the Maimed One's cane. But the genesis of the Firmament had already commenced. The rupture of the hymen had not the slightest impact on the normal progress of the Origins.

K— sometimes looked at me as though he were reading a message located somewhere between my eyes and the nape of my neck.

"We, like the universe, are fruit of the sky and the earth. My ancestors said that from the goddess's left eye was born illumination, from the right the moon, and from her nose fertility."

The boughs, the roots, the leaves of a tree—were they more eloquent than the passing days and years? S— took me shopping. He visited the shops with me but not as though he were my husband. As he adorned me was he wanting to dress himself?:

"My passion for beings of my own sex converts me into pure abstraction. What are called social problems are for me only personal conflicts. One can arrive at the heart's limit by virtue of disguise. One can find out who one most centrally is by means of an artifice."

In S— plenitude transformed gesture into rite, giving it foundation and authenticity. All his postures, all his attitudes, all his *gestes,* especially those which appeared most conventional, emanated from a unity like the light of the Firmament passing through the glass panes of the windows. Fashions, manners, modes, took root in him the way the light flooded all the greenhouse and spread through it without fluctuations.

"Now it seems someone has taken it upon himself to declare that the murderess has availed herself of the protection of the devil. I have even read that she herself is a demon in human form. As you see, we are now fully in the midst of charlatanism and magic."

Was magic an attempt to manipulate nature? Were magical rites a web of illusion? The pulse of some ineffable secret? Of the ultimate imagined reality?

"The murderess is dismissed as a visionary. We are assured that she has no contact with natural life."

Magic furnished impulse. Why could the falseness of its substance then be so clearly intuited?

"I would be so thrilled if the murderess were the devil. On another topic a certain moralist once wrote that the murderess is condemned to destroy because she herself is blighted and cankered to the very centre of her soul. He asserts that of such a person only the appearance remains. Do you see? . . . if we believed that . . . we would be faced with pure entelechy . . . yet which kills."

Could the same code of moral laws be applied to all men? Would a uniform ethical code not provoke complex problems? Would moral value then be defined by punishment and reward? By its recognition of arbitrary formulae for maintaining contractual order?

Did S— dream of eternities through which to hem in and hold evanescence?:

"The murderess is starving for victims. Do you understand why she so bewitches me? She devours them!"

Did the warrior-ants feel some existential happiness when they killed?

"But why did she never kill before? What loosed this necessity to murder?"

The Maimed One would give me boxes spilling over with decorations, certificates, medals, contracts, uniforms, dispatches. I would take them myself and carefully set them into the Constellation of the Trunks in the Firmament. When he talked to me the elder Sister paused in her reading to him of the newspaper, but the younger Sister continued squeezing out his blackheads with her fingernails.

"As soon as He dies, we are leaving. You can and should come with us. We are prepared. That is why the Keep now has every appearance of a luggage depot. It is only normal. They will not catch us unawares or unprepared."

The boxes the Maimed One gave me revolved about the Firmament in their constellations, though they seemed, when one looked at them, to be as motionless as the moon and stars.

"We are living through the worst imaginable decadence . . . the most precarious and also the most fatal. We are watching as in slow motion the new leaf is turned. The world is turning hindmost-foremost. One will be forced to make peace with the barbarians, if they catch us unprepared . . . and then later we will escape."

The Sisters prepared his medicines for him. The Maimed

One took them without moving his head. The two women oversaw the operation vigilantly, expectantly, with napkins in hand, to clean up the drops which might trickle down his lips.

"We had reached the highest peak of civilisation . . . and now before our very eyes opens the chasm. Since the moment that this decadence which paralyses our will began, all evolution in life has been closed off. Now we cannot even retrogress. We have been transformed into larvae, not to metamorphose and be reborn, but rather simply to die or allow to perish all that we had constructed in the age of triumphant enthusiasm. In the era of creation, when we still had good red blood in our veins."

The blood of the insects in the greenhouse was not red but rather colourless, or sometimes slightly green or yellow. Was that the reason ants had suffered no decay for hundreds of millions of years? Had that been why their mutations had cancelled each other out, and had these mutations constituted one element of the stability of the species? Did the unconscious life, like a great drop of liquid, imply the wild hope that one might escape fate's circle of obliteration/creation?

The Maimed One had lost his dense, opaque solidity:

"I recommend to you that you make friends among those who will be taking the reins. Begin preparing for your adaptation to life among the barbarians. You must become a member of the horde if you intend to survive."

Locusts lived a double life—they normally lived within the Firmament as solitary, peaceful insects. But suddenly they might become transformed into soldiers and join together into an army, which marched outside the walls. Their physical aspect as well as their behaviour changed. When they were solitary they were inoffensive and stable, and they partook modestly of the grass and herbs of the greenhouse. Their colour was almost indistinguishable from that of the medium in which they lived—green with brown spots and smears. But transformed into the soldiers of that army, they became bright saffron-yellow with black specks. Their legs grew more robust, more agile and athletic, their appetite immeasurably greater.

They flew in hordes, prey to an excitation which kept them from even the least moment of rest or respite. The nourishment they ingested daily might total several times their own weight. They were as much more violent and fierce as numerous in the army in which they had enrolled. They might form tidal surges of millions upon millions of locusts, laying waste to tons of vegetation each day. On joining a group, did the individual of whatever animal species or whatever human collective change aspect? Weight? Did its aggressivity augment? That spirit of gregariousness—did it lend physical strength? The instinct to be joined with others—had it replaced the instinct of self-preservation? The instinct of thought and reflexion?, that of knowledge?

The Maimed One's hysteria led him to pile his memories into huge chaotic heaps:

"My father, your grandfather, would say that if he was given a choice between a piece of bread and an onion, if he could not keep them both, then he would choose the bread, and then he would add that he liked life and he liked justice, but if he could not have them both, he would choose life."

In the Firmament, for the solitary, peaceful locusts I constructed the Garden of Grasshoppers. At its very heart was the Sanctum of the Mirror. I would destroy and rebuild it every year, precisely identical each time, with withes and sticks and splints. In its central hall I had installed a small round mirror. Locusts tempted to make the transformation into warriors might contemplate themselves in it. Did they meditate on impermanence? On the ephemeral? On the eternal?

K— wanted to be buried among thousand-year-old trees:

"One day my ashes will be a part of nature."

He wished to remain eternally in space, where silence, equilibrium, simplicity, and sobriety reigned.

"It will be the aim of my whole life."

K— described for me the route he was to follow as the itinerant hermit. Then, in silence, he concentrated. Was he meditating with closed eyes? At last he picked up a brush and wrote with rapid strokes:

I know that the butterfly flies.
I know that jellyfish swim.
I know that the ladybug eats.
But the spirit—I cannot know it.
It is in the air.
It is in the breeze.
You are like the spirit.

I WAS ON MY WAY TO THE CASTLE WITH S—. During the journey on the train I was filled with the sensation that I was not part of my body. My ears heard, my eyes saw, my movements traversed space . . . and yet everything was so far away from me!

In the dining car when I raised food to my mouth I would have the impression that someone, at some considerable distance from me, was opening my mouth and chewing.

S— sank into the dark rumen of his remembrances:

"The murderess's body is heavy to her. I know that sensation. No one has thought that perhaps she yearns to die. So then why will she not have tried suicide?"

Through the windowframe I looked out on the landscape and there came to my mind the thought that I, and all the world besides, might cease to live. Was it an idea now devoid of interest which awaited its proper and propitious moment of triumph, hourglass in hand?

"If at least I knew with certainty the murderess's age! I have the presentiment, as you know, that she is not twenty years old as she is reported to be, but rather eighteen. But even so, what has she done since puberty? Has she killed in some other way? Because it would appear evident that the murders are related to puberty. It is well-known that in the majority of women, at the onset of menstruation there is an emotional shock, a *trauma*. Is that what I felt upon discovering my own inclinations? Did this *trauma* impel her to kill? But then she would have begun killing at thirteen or fourteen years of age. Or of course one might imagine her at that age making the decision to do so . . . yet only beginning three years later! It is incongruous, though perhaps all the reactions provoked by the onset of puberty are absurd. If I had my first period I would preserve my first drops of blood; I would place them in a monstrance."

In the Park K— was sometimes overcome with debilitating attacks of laughter. He seemed so happy that his jaw flapped as he howled. Between guffaws he would say:

"I feel the same spiritual euphoria they say that mystics feel."

An automobile, a stone bench, a shoe, a toy could undam a flood of uncontainable hilarity:

"I am laughing at my own vanity. This statue of a bear is as absurd as my self-complacency. From the pedestal to the crown of its head it flaunts the image of our own self-satisfaction. The mallet and chisel, the gouge, the spatula modelled the stone millimetre by millimetre, not so that it would come to resemble a bear or a man, but rather so that it would approximate the image of our favorite fictional characters."

K— laughed so much that from time to time a stranger would ask him:

"What's gotten into you, you're laughing so hard! Your friend is so serious."

K—, at that, would laugh even more uncontrollably and his three hundred-odd pounds would quake, his eyes fill with tears of delight. Having to offer a logical reply, bounded by the limits of the reasonable, in that place at that time multiplied his howls of laughter.

When I left for the station I took my leave of the Maimed One in the Keep.

"You have done the correct thing in coming to tell your aunts and me before you leave. The last time, three years ago, when you left without telling us, we were on the point of calling the police. You were fifteen years old . . . and you simply disappeared for a week."

P—'s studio was filled with virgin canvasses, tubes of paint, brushes, paint knives. It smelled of turpentine. Standing before the easel was the television receiver, always turned on. Was it the viscous eye of the Croft? In the Keep, what function had Television taken over? Was it a centre of gravity? Of cohesion? Of suggestion? Of unjoyful splendour at the lip of the abyss of oblivion?

Time's flight oppressed the Maimed One:

"As you can see, your aunts are still filling bags and trunks. One might say the Keep has been taken over by a moving company. But in times of decadence one moves, changes residence, as though simply changing clothes, a molting . . . when nothing more can be saved or salvaged. What I sometimes feel like doing is not going on a hunger strike but rather simply stopping eating."

When the insects of the greenhouse were about to molt they stopped eating. After their fast, internal abdominal and sanguinary pressures brought on the splitting of their carapace. Once rent, it was sloughed off by means of violent spasms of contraction and expansion. When the insects were free of the old shell they swelled with air and water. Thus the new carapace, elastic only for its first few moments of exposure to the air, would harden and yet not make impossible the subsequent growth of their body. In the greenhouse did the insects feel responsible for each and every one of their molecules, and those of the Firmament as well?

The mists of augury blurred the Maimed One's sight and gave him a kind of ecstatic vision:

"What is to come will stucco us in so tight, will armour us so stiff, that we will not be able to breathe."

In the dining car the translucent goblet allowed me to see the liquid it contained. The light swaying of the train broke the form of the liquid into sparkling bubbles and tiny waves of surf.

S— could not seem to see how at once simple and complex a glass of water might be:

"The prevailing opinion of the news commentators is that she murders every man with whom she goes to bed. I understand that perfectly. After a night of sexual drunkenness, of humiliations, tears, mud, who would not wish he could destroy the person who was present at his ruin? The murderess, one might very easily suppose, was with a man, for the first time in her life, on the floor of the Cinema between the two last rows of seats. And this man was the goatish old landowner."

A drop of water fell onto the tablecloth and stayed there round and full. I merged into it, far removed from the flight of the landscape. I could not distinguish between the exterior and the interior of the droplet. I could hear, in that limbo of transincarnation, S—'s voice—without listening to it. I felt time pass neither in the self-destruction of its seconds nor in the eternal persistence of the instant. Was it this last sensation which K— enjoyed when he offered his thanks before the centuries-old sequoia? K— ended his meditation by clapping his hands together:

"A state of inspired impotence paralysed me. . . . I did not know where I was . . . where the world was . . . where my spirit was."

Radiant with happiness K— resembled an insect just issued from the larval stage:

"When I utter the words I utilize when I speak to you, thousands of thoughts traverse my spirit. I see myself at every stage of my journey back to my country. I am hen and egg, painting and image, smoke and fire, water and wet."

Seated in the compartment, motionless but running through the landscape, I had the feeling of flying between the window and the horizon, above the train's engine, above the clouds, among constellations and the void. It was a sensation I could neither communicate nor note down. An urging-forward held back and savoured as ardent desire.

S— refined away his doubts by going more and more deeply into conjecture:

"There is one thing the official investigation has established with certainty—the murderess did not lose her virginity that first night she killed. The laboratory found that the victim ejaculated before dying. I would venture to say he did so at the moment his throat was cut. The laboratory tests would have found traces of the murderess's blood . . . had there been any. Therefore the murderess was not a virgin. However, on the other hand it is inconceivable that a man could have deflowered her before that night without thereby bringing on his own death automatically. Therefore, the murderess took her own maidenhead, herself. . . . I am convinced of that. With her own hands, her own fingers, perhaps with the help of some domestic object which had some significance for her, such as the leg of a chair which the fornicator who engendered her had sat in, or still sits in."

The wheels of the train, with their unending and systematic clacking, led me to levels of understanding I had never before imagined. Did everything seem more real than before? And yet at the same time, was everything my eyes perceived mere images of sublimation?

On a whim S— digressed:

"For the murderess the life-giving explosion of ejaculation is death's ally."

In the dining car the emanations of the earth, the echoes of the universe transported me as though I were a feather in a hurricane.

"Life and death. Good and evil. Murderess and victim."

In the Firmament, the Assembly of the Incarnation, so as to resolve conflicts between insects or to reduce discords brought about by schisms, adopted the following statement of principle:

"Only unity exists. It will be known under diverse names, as a proof of wisdom."

S— wove a motley fabric of arcane deductions:

"Human beings are infinitely disappointing to the murderess. . . . Perhaps she prefers animals. The world for her is vile, horrible, ugly . . . yet it cannot besmirch her. I wonder if she doesn't stay on the margins somehow of her murders. I believe I live them with more interest than she does."

I watched the procession of the landscape past the window, knowing I could not halt it. When I saw something lovely with

K— I wanted it to stay that way always. Was that happiness evidence of a flight outside time?

K— gave me an hourglass, which I set up in the Desert of Space in the greenhouse:

"Outside time there is only eternity."

On the upper crown I inscribed a maxim, as a testament to his words:

"Time does not exist. The image held of it is a seed of eternity."

A worm got into the upper chamber. Did it want to be the effigy of past time? To symbolize the present?

S— knew nothing about cold, emotionless outbursts:

"The murderess has known and slit the throats of three men. She spoke with them, but she did not maintain a true conversation. I am persuaded that she studied them like butterflies impaled on a pin. She observed them as I at times have done with men—I only feel curiosity for the mechanics of excitation. The police have proven that the first time, in the Cinema, she and the stranger lay on the floor. He beneath her. Naturally. He tumbled down between the seats to receive her. I can imagine her looking down at him, studying that mass of excited flesh by the faint flickering light of the screen, like a woman who dissects before killing."

The Firmament was full of mysteries not to be elucidated by congresses or assemblies or schismatic sects. I felt them, pleasures which plunged me outside time. Intelligence could not begin to fathom them. I was captivated by them, little shining circular enigmas which never suffered eclipses.

"For me woman is wetness, rents, softness, voids. But I cannot resign myself to seeing the murderess in that light. Those who say she is the devil know, perhaps, that Satan signifies shadow. That is, the deformation projected by the sun. What does in fact seem likely is that she behaves like the serpent of Paradise. She smiles serenely. She listens as though she were promising the Tree of Good and Evil—the Good and the Evil of Pleasures without End."

So as to avoid confusion, the knots of energy which slept in the common ground of the Firmament were defined. They were at the disposal of all—crane-flies, miller-beetles, maxims, borer-worms, monuments, mountain ranges. It little mattered, for example, to know whether the Vat had been in the greenhouse since the Maimed One's childhood, as legend had it, or whether it had been installed in the more recent years so as to represent his role in things. The knots tied to the tangle infused some measure of assurance, confidence, certainty into the muddle of this present we inhabited.

S— was ebullient, shining like a lighthouse against the gloom of the myriad pain that lay all about:

"What must the love life, the life of the senses of the landholder have been like, with his seven grown children, when he met up with the murderess? He believed in the devil, in a monster-shaped monster like the dragon of the subconscious, and he meets a beautiful woman impavid, implacable, and *suave*. The defeat was implicit in the terms of the battle. I, rather than killing him at the end, would have bitten him 'hind the neck as I possessed him. Ah, you see, all of this excites me, I must confess. The lower portion of the spine is called the sacrum, to show the sacred mystery the anal region encloses. What celestial music is imprisoned in this cloacal vault of secrets?"

The insects of the greenhouse could emit sounds produced by rubbing their antennae or their legs or their wings together. In these sounds one might glimpse the path leading from them to the words of today. Thousands of years before the Firmament, the first women who tried to emit significant sounds associated a particular significance with the way they moved their mouths or breathed. When they were frightened or wanted to smash something they produced M's. They pressed their lips together, expelled air through their noses, and made their vocal cords vibrate. They imitated crickets. The urge to speak, say, gave form to the sound, which later fell ignored on the fringes of the phrase.

S— spilled over into details:

"The murderess seduces with an intoxicating music. Serenity! In reality she achieves with it a combustion that burns like a tongue of fire. To gain some idea of it one would have to imagine the buzz of an angel-bee or the hiss of a devil-serpent. The victims, so as to hear this enchanting, intoxicating melody, not only opened the porches of their ears but every orifice and pore of their bodies. The postman to forget the obsessive memory of his former lover. To betray himself at the moment he believes he has entered, newly wed to the murderess, the Boulevard of Happiness."

Music, according to legend, brought about the spiritual unification of the Firmament. At night when I would lie on the rush mat and sing, my voice would seem to grow wings. It would trace musical scrolls and volutes in the air, curvetting away to infinity. The beauty of the melody would depend upon the participation of my body, my breathing, my emotions. The hymn was the flag of sound planted on the island of harmony.

Did life, for S—, unravel at the blurry edges?:

"The victim is a matter of indifference to the murderess. He is like a reed flute—she plays it to find what sound it makes and then she breaks it in two."

When we stepped down from the train S— rented a car to take us to the Castle:

"D— has invited depraved couples. Those are his terms. Depravity, dream, ecstasy, he has said time and time again, are means of approaching worlds governed by radically different laws."

In the Temple of the Design procreation might supposedly be achieved without concupiscence, thanks to insects which were born without *trauma*. A spiritual polygamy was contemplated, to be brought about by means of inviolable accords or contracts. A deep moat always filled with water isolated the Temple from the rest of the Firmament. According to legend, the walls of the Temple enclosed only chimeras, illusions, errors, and fevered vagaries.

ON THE EVENING BEFORE THE PARTY D— greeted us, S— and me, at the Castle. The walls of the *salon* were covered with paintings and *objets de vertu*.

In the greenhouse camel-crickets produced a certain kind of music, white flies executed various courting dances, murderer-ants drummed on the abdomens of their plant-louse slaves as they waited, self-absorbed, to see their sweet excrement emerge. The artistic impulses of the insects of the Firmament—what limits did they have? Did they give up to, recognise the superiority of, all they did not know?

S—, in spite of having meticulously prepared everything, seemed tentative and doubtful in D—'s presence. Was he embarrassed? Frightened?

"The truth is . . . that she is not my slave."

D—'s eyes opened round as saucers. He waved his arms. His gestures portrayed ire with great artifice and virtuosity:

"How dare you, sir, employ the biblical word 'slave' then in our correspondence? . . . Though I must admit that ruses, tricks, and lies please me, with their quality of the sacred."

S— looked indirectly and somewhat sheepishly at him. Bewildered?

I had observed in the insect colonies of the greenhouse that a maladjusted individual's altruism shrivelled. Could it foresee, though impotent to avoid, its own destruction?

"I beg you, my Fair Maiden, to show me how you masturbate this gentleman in private."

S— took my hands and said to D—:

"But you must know . . . D— . . . that I practise . . . chastity!"

D—, enchanted, raised his arms ceilingward as though giving thanks to the chandelier.

"How perfect! In an anti-materialistic orgy like this one which the divinity will allow us to celebrate tomorrow night, we most imperiously need the tantalizing figure of the Chaste Male. You will represent that figure among the depraved."

We went with D— to a restaurant to eat. He was for the entire evening in a state of acute tension. The energy he manifested was more surprising for its constancy than for its intensity. At no moment did it wane or take refuge in rest or respite. How many hours of dynamic force could he command? The cycles of activity/repose of the insects in the greenhouse were regular. Most individuals did not begin to be active until well along in the morning, and their period of rest, which lasted until the next day, began just at dusk. Others, contrariwise, such as moths and cockroaches, awoke at midnight and by dawn had already returned to their nests and crannies. No species had a period of activity in excess of ten hours.

"In this cretinous and cretinizing century a genius such as myself and a Fair Maiden such as yourself are considered to be beings perfectly similar to the common run of mortals. When will they ever learn that we digest, hear, fart, and think in ways singular, unique, and inimitable. And singular, unique, and inimitable too are our fingernails and the other horny places of our bodies, our urine, our sweat. Irrefutably different from that of the rest of humanity. I suppose, Fair Maiden, that you are religious."

S— attempted to reply for me, but D— barged on:

"My first teacher taught me to blaspheme. He would affirm that blasphemy was the loveliest gem of our language. A thousand times he would repeat to me that religion is woman's stuff. That is why today I am perfervidly religious, as my moustache shows, which curls upward to heaven as symbol of the upright mysticism of ascension. Learn to hate and abhor, Fair Maiden mine, great fallen moustaches, which point downward depressingly, catastrophically, *nibelungenliches,* snot-dripping and befogged. My Dionysiac superman has been supplanted by my brilliant superwoman of genius, as homage to my idolatred wife."

D— never repressed his passions. He held them in suspense so as to avoid their completely leaking away. He grasped them at the very root and hilt. Hopping gnats and banded moths also seemed tumultuous, frenetic in the greenhouse. At nearby tables the diners were observing D—. Aversion and anger were more noticeable among them than curiosity or delighted amusement. Some commented aloud. The words *clown, contemptible, business person, shameless, wretched, commercial, riffraff* were heard. D— seemed fully conscious of them, and indifferent:

"I do not defy the hostile world with heroism but rather with the attitude that my life is a work of art."

When D— said that he would take me to his studio to make a sketch of me, S— seemed to look at me helpless and abandoned. What sort of cerebral perturbations provoked that emotion in him? Was it the automatic mechanisms of perception that led him to uneasiness and anxiety? And was that in turn propagated into descents into fits of glowering and brow-beetling shot across from time to time by horribly painful despairs?

I reclined motionless on the *chaise longue* in D—'s studio. The workshop was a small *salon* with naked walls and two high windows. An enormous canvas, resting on two easels, divided the room in two. Behind the frame of the canvas D—, invisible, was drawing. Often his head bobbed out from the right edge as he studied me. As the sun poured in on me I could hear the rasping of D—'s charcoal frenetically lining and hatching the cloth, as if it were the edge of a sword.

"My dear Fair Maiden, I should suggest that you undress completely. Your naked body will produce an immediate pleasure in me. You will be able to judge its intensity for yourself by the amount of saliva that appears in the corners of

my mouth and on my lips. Mixing and joining the two para-
noid and ecstatic pleasures of painting and contemplating your
nude body cannot fail to make me drool in torrents."

As I undressed with my eyes closed, I felt that I was in the
Firmament on my *tatami* mat. My natural spontaneity—would
it suddenly appear—an impulse, the impulse that sparked
my thinking? Would it materialize at all? Did it come and
go depending on whether it felt protected and secure? Overcoming then the fragility which too would have its sudden
eruptions? In the interior of my body all was intercommunicat-
ing—my lungs with my eyes, my kidneys with my nose, my
spleen with my mouth, my liver with my ears. I could perceive
how I absorbed the gusty breath of the Firmament through my
mouth and lungs and returned it through the streams of light
which were pouring out from my eyes as I glanced about.

D— cawed in his private whirl of energy:

"*Cock-a-doodle-doo!* That piercing cockcrow you just heard
helps me to externalise my emotions. How thankful I am
to the All-powerful for never having made me fond of that
dust-laden product of castrating materialism—modern art.
My erotic concerns are aimed at the destruction of utopias.
Geometers and builders of utopias never find their sex hard.
Speaking of which, I am somewhat indisposed by a violent
erection."

In the external organs—mouth, ears, eyes, nose—did there
reside the material basis of knowledge? And the internal organs—did they serve to concentrate and protect life? Like the
roots of trees? Did they guarantee the existence of the Firmament? Without them would the minnows have died in the Vat
and the sun-spiders pose motionless in the hammock of their
webs until they perished?

Was D— squandering his apogeal moment?:

"I impose upon myself the task of meticulously drawing,
one by one, the hairs which adorn your pubis so as to maintain
the stupefying, burning prickle of my carnal pleasure. Can you
spiritually feel my lead as it traces the external orifice of your
womb across the canvas?"

I was reposing in the void as though I were lying in the heart of the universe. What was it that lent colour to the infinite beings of the greenhouse? What storms or revels? What clinking of glasses or bells broadcast hues, tints, tones, spectra, polychromy throughout the creation?

"The sketch, my Fairest Maiden, of your naked body would reach the highest flights of beatific prodigy if your participation might be dressed out with convulsive and spasmodic touches. I advise you to take advantage of your nudity and of the fact that I am looking at you with foul concupiscence by masturbating. You should do so with the forefinger of your right hand. I should be grateful if the expression on your face, thanks to this manipulation, should resemble that of the female anchorite who, after a week of fasting, eats a grasshopper. Your attitude should reproduce that of the mystic consuming the Supreme Being."

Did serpent-flies know Good and Evil? Did they only act prudently in the face of the complexity of the Real? Was the art of living, for them, a technique of the heart for not losing the vital principle? Did they not express the Known? Did they not know what they expressed? Did they grope? Did they balance their distant anxieties with sterile desolation?

"A Fair Maiden masturbating celebrates the Mystery of the Assumption."

What meaning could be given to D—'s jumble of words?

"The superwoman, alone, at the culmination of her will, ascends into heaven. The orgasm which her spiritual potency triggers in her responds to the simplest laws of Physics. Keep masturbating, my dear Fair Maiden."

I tried to think of nothing. And yet my thoughts, flowing independently, ran over into the everyday paths of analysis with their circumconvolutions and labyrinthine sinuosities. My thoughts crossed mountains and valleys, countries and regions, memories and desires.

"Do you know, Fairest Maiden, what I am doing here behind the veil of the canvas while you caress yourself? . . . You cannot see me here behind my screen? . . . Can you not guess?

. . . Together we are living an instant of complete fulfilment.
. . . I also am ascending materially and gloriously into heaven.
I am stiff and erect as I, like you, rise. I levitate. I feel more
a woman than ever in my life."

K— said that writing was drawing. A written maxim figured
forth, for him, both the pictorial and the poetic expression.
When in his beautiful calligraphy he wrote me messages did
he identify himself not only with the content but also with the
form? Was every line and flourish of every letter passed
through the sieve of his heart? Had the Written Word been
changed into the Shining of the Heart? Into resplendent,
sumptuous balance cradling colour, line, attitude, feeling, serenity, precision, glory? It vibrated like his breathing and held
the very rhythm of his life. Before I took the train K— had
written me:

> You will see new mountains, new fields, new rivers,
> new landscapes.
> Be conscious of their essential characters and you will
> be able to praise them with your spirit and admire them
> with your eyes.

For months K— had been wanting to paint the sequoia in
the Park. He thought of that whenever he was in its presence,
or in the silence of his studio, or in the tumult of streets and
boulevards. But he could never capture its essence:

"I was meditating yesterday. Last night. The moment I lit
the oil lamp I saw it. At last I *had* the sequoia. I could not paint
it without following the itinerary which will lead me from the
sequoia in the Park to the sequoia itself within my soul. The
tree shows its essence to my eyes, my eyes to my heart, my
heart to my brush."

Was it, for K—, the dynamism of nature that inspired calligraphy? Did he trace those signs so as to identify with nature?
Was K— aware of the incessant windings, inevitable and
exact, which his virtuoso nib followed?

"Calligraphy is not satisfied by the simple lines of letters and symbols. It is dynamic. And it is also an adventure, a dance. Each word in calligraphy has its particular rhythm, each line obeys a special choreography."

When K— wrote out a maxim was he inhabited or possessed by the entire universe? He composed it once and only once. Serenely, with no hesitation or doubt, and without retouching. Was the connexion between emotional well-being, thought, and phrase so intimate? Between the model, the heart, and the hand? Between the maxim and the paper? When he wrote in that flowing calligraphy of his, he was more tranquil and at peace than at any other time. Could he forget that he was creating? At that instant, could he closet himself within himself? Did K— wish by the calligraphy to reveal his most intimate self to me?

"Nature comes to me."

Did K— not feel the distance between the object and the subject? Did he do away with the space-time relationship?

"I return to virgin land."

Did he delve, dive, into the universe so as to define the indefinable? K— imposed nothing, defined nothing. The ultimate secret of life, for him—was it the peace at the centre of the universe? The infinite suddenly clustered about one single moment of stunned astonishment?

D—'s voice pulled me up out of my memories and deposited me again on the *chaise longue:*

"You and I are performing an amazing act. It is the proof that I have arrived at the apex of my genius. Separated by the virgin veil of the painting, by the immaculate hymen of the canvas, we are, nonetheless, joined by lasciviousness . . : yet five yards distant from one another. We will not break that maidenhead or stain it. We are joined by and voluptuously damned to solitary pleasure. I too, my Fair Maiden, I too am masturbating. And as I do each time I perform a brilliant, unique act, I hear the hoarse, sweetly muted voice of my friend the murdered poet, urging me on from On High— *Olé!*"

As I continued doing with the forefinger-of-my-body what D— wished me to, I recalled that, in the greenhouse, a wasp could go on cleaning its forelegs for hours after it was decapitated.

A S THROUGH THE WINDOW OF OUR chamber I contemplated the horizon, hushed within its own soft denseness of space, of proportion, of reserve, of silence, S— painted my toenails a light mauve.

"I was listening to the radio while you were with D—. In the library of the Conservatory a cigarette paper has been found with a phrase written on it by the murderess: 'How can one know the shape of all the signs and clews?' It is written very curiously. According to the police, in a strange but coherent calligraphy. Every newspaper and magazine has published a photograph of the rolling paper. What a shame that newspapers arrive so late at the Castle! How I would love to look at, touch, sniff at her handwriting!"

Instead of leaving it for the next day, S— preferred to prepare the dresses, the pomades, the perfumes, the shoes, the creams and lotions for the party on the day before it. He laid the clothes out on the bed and looked at them indecisively.

"Tomorrow morning it will be I who bathes you, depilates you, plucks your eyebrows, and shaves your head again. I will do all of it as though . . . I were . . . YOU."

According to one legend, before the death of the gardener there was a flood in the greenhouse. All the insects perished, drowned. The only insects saved were a few pairs who took refuge in a tortoise shell. When the waters withdrew, these couples reconstituted life within the greenhouse. From that moment on, the roots of ignorance in the Firmament were extirpated and the thirst for what was lacking was assuaged, all things humbly conformed to palpable reality.

"An expert at handwriting analysis says that he is certain that the murderess's handwriting reveals a vigorous temperament, an alert intelligence, and a combative, highly active nature. I agree with everything except the combativeness. I picture her firm but not self-assertive. As one might expect, the charlatan runs with the pack—he pretends that when he deciphered the signs of each word and phrase he had an impression of unease and even of terror when he saw how the murderess conceived order and morality. Ta-da-da-*dum*-de-*dum!* Naturally, he affirms that she is a woman lacking neither in firmness nor in intuition. The point at which he and I most diverge is her age. He maintains that it is the handwriting of a woman near thirty, while I give her a maximum of eighteen years. He states that she is dynamic, daring, and has great initiative—as of course she has amply demonstrated by, according to him, the synthesis of oriental and occidental calligraphic hands she employs."

The sun seemed, in but a few moments, to slide from my head down to my knees. Sitting on the small balcony, I felt the rays striking me horizontally just before they disappeared altogether. Everything seemed the manifestation of that glowing splendour—the noise and bustle of the birds, S—'s bustle behind me, the sound of a stone dropped or fallen, the trickling rush of the water in the fountain. Was I meditating over a ray of sunlight? Or was that red ray of sunlight itself my meditation? Was I thinking about where I was? I perceived an illumination spontaneous, cool, ineffable, which came from a closed, radiant world. The light bathed me, entered me, emanated from me. Did nothing change? Had everything already changed? Was there no unconsciousness, unconscious? Only the perpetual permutation of subjects, fate's eternal return masked behind the harlequin *façade* of chance?

"Apparently the police are searching for the murderess in oriental-language schools. Because of the calligraphy. How ridiculous. Can anyone imagine the murderess sitting at a desk in a schoolroom taking a language class? What in fact *might* have occurred is that she is somehow connected to a foreigner who by osmosis has transmitted to her the art of writing. There cannot be many such people. That seems to be a more serious trail to follow, thanks to which the net may start to close in around the murderess."

The ray of sunlight was just on the point of disappearing. Nothing lasted beyond a whisper, everything was renewed from instant to instant. Without actually forming any idea, I thought about my body, K—'s body, earth, water, wind, fire, the circle of nothingness, the circle of knowledge. . . . Then I thought about nothing. I held my lucidness intact, and I kept myself from questioning too closely what was inward and what was outward. A circular glow surrounded the afternoon and then embraced it.

The Marquis entered our chamber:

"If I do not see her tonight she will go mad. I don't know whether she can bear it. It has been three days since she knew where I was. I have her below . . . well tied up. I want her to live this imprisonment like a hell. Come with me, the two of you. Accompany me."

That night I dreamt of another universe, the inverted image of that which existed. When in that universe the sun rose, it set in this one; its day was our night; its summer, our winter; rivers ran upstream to their sources; peaks became valleys; love, hate; charity, meanness. I journeyed through that inverse universe listening to a voice say, "Go back to the light." I wandered in ecstasy through space in that inverted universe, convinced that I was on my way to the centre of the cosmos. Enraptured by inspiration, I flew. I returned at sunset in all the pleasure of certainty. In such a straitly enclosed place there was room for only the most telling proofs.

We went down into the crypt. The Marquis seemed fascinated by the routine.

"The night I met her she whispered in my ear, 'Do with me what you will. I am your chattel.' I had always dreamt of owning a slave, like the Romans, tied at my command with a rope binding her ankles to her neck, as I had seen in an encyclopaedia as a child. 'I will be your slave if you but ask it of me.' . . . 'I will await you day and night, chained in the mud.' . . . It was she who suggested the idea to me. I asked her to repeat aloud what she had whispered in my ear . . . so that everyone could hear. When she spoke a cramp convulsed my entire body. One of the diners grew furious with her; she took her aside and told her it was shameful to behave in such a way, to exhibit herself thus. 'You have no right to force me to take part in your *macabre* perversions.' She responded very coolly that she loved me and that she could only be happy as my object, my thing, my sacrificial animal . . . that that for her was a life of love. I became so excited that we didn't make it to the bed.''

What were the relations that branched into what was called love? For K—, the union of lover and loved was effected at two levels, one external and sensual and the other internal and spiritual. The song of love was a hymn to everyone, to everything. Therefore when the lover and the loved entwined it was an allusion to heaven, to the sun, the moon, the stars, valleys, flowers, cedar trees, the seagull's flight, frost. The universe was made coterminous with love. Without privileging anything or excluding anything, lovers unified all nature, thanks to amorous knowledge. For K—, was the consequence of loving one person in particular that one loved all people in some singular way? Did he consider the beloved a model of the soul itself beckoned to love? The amorous dialogue was for him a sacred dance presided over by a harmony at last recovered. When he said goodbye to me as I was about to board the train, K— mused over the phases of this choreography:

''When a couple momentarily draws apart, the partner who is in love is the one who suffers. And seeks out the other ever more ardently. The lover caresses the idea of groaning at the drama of separation. . . . The lover lacks the love that nourishes him.''

For the Marquis, was the spirit alone and single? With no

hope at all? Did it silently harbour in the fog and mist its daily and nightly rancours and complaints?

"We spent the first night in my bedroom. The next morning I took her down to the crypts in the abandoned cellar of the Castle. It is a place always warm by virtue of the furnace located nearby. I locked her up in the last cell. I have the only key. I stripped off her clothes and tied her by the neck as though she were a colt. She kissed my hands as I worked. I spent that day at my office, excited, thinking of her. I knew she was awaiting me, that I was the only person alive who could open the padlocked cell door and sate her. I imagined her naked lying in the straw. With every passing minute her ardour for my return was growing . . . she was more and more aroused . . . as was I. That night, when I unlocked the lock . . . I had never felt such raging, boiling agitation. . . . I could not imagine that two human beings could couple with such overwhelming, ecstatic fury."

At night K— would escort me to the Rose Garden:

"The eyes of night are stars. Bright celestial bodies adorn the wings of night."

What did the dimension of night represent for K—? The nightwatch that sculpts soft eyes of jet?

"Night entombs us in its immensities."

Had K— discovered its harmony, its rhythm?:

"Night breaks my bonds. It frees me."

Was he nostalgic for the invisible? Did he believe that there could be no fairer voyage than that voyage undertaken to our own inward lands? At night Death inspired in him no terrors. For K— there was no contrast between Life and Death, light and darkness. Did he love the visible and the invisible equally?:

"During the night all is relation, love, the interchange of secrets, fulfilment, plenitude."

When we came to the crypt, the Marquis asked S— and me not to make any sound as we watched the Captive through the peephole. She was enchained by a thick ring about her neck. Her eyes were open. She was lying on a heap of straw. We contemplated her in silence. She was young and beautifully sensuous.

"I am here! Behind the door. . . . I have brought two friends with me. . . . They wanted to see you. . . . They are now contemplating you as though they had come to the Zoological Gardens."

"Come close, I beg you. . . . How long has it been since the last time you came?"

"Three days. . . . You will give me pleasure before these friends. I want to show them how I have tamed you."

"Come, then. . . . What unspeakable anguish one feels . . . waiting without hope. . . . I have not slept for a single moment in anticipation of hearing your voice."

"You are in heat!"

"I have cried out. No one came, or answered. I felt I was drowning in an abyss of solitude."

"Can you not stop loving me?"

"Have mercy!"

"No."

"When one suffers so . . . to the last extreme of pain . . . I feel I am sinking slowly into myself. . . ."

"It excites me to know that you have suffered, and even more to know that you have wept."

The Marquis was speaking through the door. Did he shrink at turning the lock? What might be deduced from the Captive's behaviour? What features of her intuition or her inheritance had led her to lend herself to this situation? Did she require some special physical vigour? Some strategy by which forms of paradoxical altruism would be stimulated? Was she, in her motivations, comparable to the plant-louse enslaved to the leaf-cutter ant? The subjective pleasure its domination gave the louse—was that pleasure greater than the pain of the tortures inflicted on it by the ant?

"I look for nothing outside you. . . . I abandon myself to the pleasure of discovering how to love madly."

"In that case, you have not suffered so much."

"I deserve your punishments. I have no right to object to them."

In the Era of Appearances, one schism in the Firmament defended the idea that science had spiritual significance. One assembly at last declared that the world of subjective truth and the lying world of objectivity were mutually exclusive, that perfection was inaccessible in the real world. According to this doctrine, then, one did not arrive at knowledge by reason but rather by awe. The rapture of a burning sensationalism inspired existences without rest or relief.

The Captive and the Marquis entwined about each other like two rhinoceros beetles. Then they penetrated one another with the wild frenzy of two rat-tail larvae. They looked like prisoners in some invisible spider's-web. Together they made sounds like pharaoh termites. She, on her own, emitted a sound like that of the common cicada; he, like that of a bumblebee in June. There were moments when they lay immobile, expectant, like two metallic lizards. Like two Siamese fighting-fish they caressed each other from head to fins, their loins quivering. Their bodies were covered with mud and muck like dung-beetles. They dripped saliva. Were they drooling like oozing seedpods? Were they sawing with their extremities like the praying mantis? From time to time they would scream—which one of them?—like a cobra.

Meanwhile, S— distractedly stared at me. I saw that he was imagining another sort of make-up for my face.

The postures and positions adopted by the Captive and the Marquis—were they the postures most favourable to asceticism? To the awakening of energy? Did they use their voices as insignificant accompaniment? As an aid to the externalising of latent energies? Did they dilate their receptive capacities? Soon they adopted a different rhythm. Panting and asthmatic. Were they trying thereby to get past the obstacles which stood in the way of the goal they were seeking? Did viscous, wet desire rear invisible over their cast-down control and propriety? Over fallen dignity?

The Captive and the Marquis formed figures which recalled an infinity of natural or artful acts. They seemed two newly born creatures with the bones still unformed, unjelled, two wild beasts without claws or teeth, two poisonous insects milked of all their venom, two bawling calves, two impotent nonagenarians.

In the greenhouse a geography of suffering was created with hieroglyphics scrawled on the ground as spiritual emblems. Was there, beneath every pain, a symbol?

K— rejected the dichotomy of soul and body. For him, soul was simply the animating principle. There could be no duality without unity.

"The body is not the prison of the soul—nor the tool of transgression. It is sacred. It emanates from the universe and is a reflexion of it. It directly and spontaneously participates in the essence of the universe."

Did K— for that reason respect other men's bodies and his own?

The Captive and the Marquis, like two drugged crickets, like two butterflies of the devil stripped of their wings, writhed in convulsions. To show me the eternal essence of which my body was formed—and which I so wished not to know anything of? To show me the volcanoes and the *massifs* of absolute, insensible, and irrational perpetuity?

ON THE MORNING OF THE PARTY, I observed, when I awoke, my body lying on the bed. When I sat up, my spine grew straight and erect and resumed its normal suppleness. In the silence and immobility of the morning, I consciously controlled my two lungs lying next to my spine. They breathed. My lower belly hung from my pelvis as though it were the bag of a foetus. My blood circulated, watering my brain, my glands, my organs. Why did my body suggest unexplained problems to me? Why did I not want to confront them? Confront each cell doing, like an atom, its own secret work? Was each molecule somehow my body? My body, alteration? Alteration, manifested in the universe's abundant stuff?

Was the Firmament eternal? Was the answer to be found in my vertebral column? Did the path which guided my existence lie under my feet?

That night, some guests arrived in a yacht. D— greeted them:

"Your lord- and ladyships—the party will begin in one hour. The signs are excellent. This morning, at eleven-thirty, I bathed for a long while in a sea as trembling as an olive grove. I closed my eyes and could imagine myself swimming in a liquid composed of tears and of mercury. Last night I dreamt of a sea covered with every conceivable pastel hue. I have intensely lived each and every moment of this morning. We will be present this night at the nuclear triumph of the

Dionysiac-Satanic feast which we will share to the greater glory of God."

The broad vaulted cellar of the Castle was dominated by the transparent walls of an open swimming pool set in the centre of the space. Guests swam in the central patio. When they dived, naked as tadpoles, I contemplated them through the plastic walls in the basement. Did they remind me of the complex dynamics of the amphibians? Of the perfection of an exact, tiny being rescued from undersea suffering?

"I wish to announce, your highnesses, that this Fair Maiden and myself, performed, yesterday, after lunch, an act of cybernetic sex. We gave shape to one of my megalomaniac dreams."

The great cellar of the Castle opened onto several niches and grottoes. Each one of them had three or four straw pallets on the floor.

"We joined together as in courtly love, virginally, impalpably. We were five yards apart in my studio. The nucleic acid of our coupled orgasms, by the grace of that distance that linked them, was transmuted into the breath of archangels."

From the direction of the great tower of the Castle there arrived an ancient, obese gentleman with long white locks of hair depending from the fringe around his ears, under an otherwise completely bald dome. In his right hand he was carrying a long crop and in his left the ends of several lengths of chain. He walked erect, imperiously, like a blue bottlefly. The chains were attached to five large rings which circled the neck, wrists, and ankles of a very tall, dark, well-proportioned young man who was barefoot but dressed in midnight-blue breeches. He walked with his head bowed. He at once obeyed the orders of the old man leading him. Did there exist some transmigration of inaccessible desire to inconfessable disappointment? Did the shadows swell in their pristine gloom?

"Your lord- and ladyships, the party will begin at midnight exactly. I beg you to begin taking your places. When you speak to me, I should remind you that you must call me Divine One."

Couples were entering now through the fortified gates. The guards and sentinels of the Castle blocked entry to the crowds of the uninvited. Invective, jeering, shouts could be heard.

The Maimed One would say that everything would change, that the unleashed hordes would destroy centuries of civilisation:

"This decadence we are living through has been written in the very nature of the achievements we have sought and won. Suddenly, we open our eyes and find ourselves surrounded by barbarian hordes. Our customs, our morals, our modes of behaviour have been taken over. All that is lacking is to finish off the little that is left of our essence. But they'll never catch *me.*"

S— finally introduced himself to D— as my slave. The Marquis held the Captive, naked and on all-fours, on a leash beside him like a show dog. In the Castle tumult reigned—the buzz of a funeral? Why did I have the impression of being surrounded by death? Why was a cloud, a bird, a voice enough to put the wide borders of the sky in place?

A paralysed old man, in his wheelchair, crossed the drawbridge jeered at by the mob on the outside. He was painted, from his bald pate downward, in a motley, clashing, shocking, feminine manner. A mauve-tinted tulle veil partly covered his body. He was pushed along by an adolescent girl who looked as though she had been plucked alive from a volcano, so covered was her naked body in ash and lava.

When I buried an insect in the Firmament, death went before, as perfume the flower of white ginger. As a flame which flared up from my very contemplation of the corpse.

In the morning S— relived the Soirées as he plucked out my hair for the party:

"The police have new clews now, after analysing the cigarette paper and ink with which the maxim was written and which they found in the Conservatory. The murderess used a purple Chinese ink, called, as you may know, but erroneously, India ink. . . . The colour is most unusual. The product is sold in only seven shops. They are asking questions of the clerks and salespeople in those shops now. Something serious at last. The salesclerk may very well remember an attractive young woman who buys or bought purple India ink. Imagine—this has been going on for years. She is a regular client. . . . What could be more probable under the circumstances. Therefore, the police will find out the area in which she lives. And once that is found out . . . The noose begins to tighten."

In the greenhouse I would give a breadcrumb to lost earwigs, repair flour-beetles' shells with rubber cement, and fish fallen baby crickets out of the Vat. To feel the weight of suffering of insects and human beings, could one use a scale so delicate that the wing of a pygmy moth would tip it? Was the caught breath of a pang the stellar cirrus wind of our own reality?

S— revelled in the enigmas and meanderings of his investigation:

"They have discovered a sliver of steel embedded between two vertebrae in the caretaker's body. They deduce from that that it is a fragment from the murderess's razor. So far as I am concerned it is confirmation of my thesis that the murderess did not murder the caretaker at all, but that the porter did, with a violent, harsh slash, because the murderess sweetly slices throats . . . with not the least trace of violence. Without a struggle. The police laboratory has determined that the razor is a straight razor of an old design which is no longer marketed. And that in its day it could only be bought abroad. How has it come into her possession? The murderess never steals or robs. Theft would never enter her mental designs. Therefore we must ask—who has given her such a strange object? No one, of course, in her family. . . . Although I picture her solitary, alone, it is just possible that she has a common run-of-the-mill garden-variety father or grandfather—which means, of course, that he will be a man incapable of giving such an object to a daughter or granddaughter. The most reasonable thing to assume is that she made a trip abroad. She met a very unusual man who gave her as a *souvenir*—a straight razor! An old man who had used it years ago . . . a curious, provocative, strange, unconventional creature—an artist, let us say. A novelist or a poet, or, better yet, a painter or sculptor who would know the value of *objets*. Probably . . . a plastic artist who was old enough to be her grandfather or great-grandfather and who presented her with the razor as a unique, uncommon gift, beautiful for him, personal, filled with memories. He would have wished to surprise, perhaps shock, her, to do something unexpected, unforgettable, which would be forever engraved on her memory—and so he gave her a razor. The razor he shaved with as a young man. Perhaps he wanted to shock himself, wake himself up, as well."

The body—was it nothing but the flicker of an image on a movie screen, deduced from the whisper of hope? Time—did it tick so as to push away and set at a distance, so as then to unite?

"To summarize—At this moment, thanks to new clews and my own inquiries, I have several pieces of evidence: the murderess travelled abroad, met a plastic artist, probably a painter or a sculptor. This 'original', this 'character', this strange and provocative artist was or is a very very old man who gave her the barber's straight razor with which he had shaved when he was a young man. I also know that the murderess is eighteen years old, although she looks somewhat older, that she is beautiful, even 'sexy', and that she has a sort of halo of placidness or sweetness—nothing fazes her. She currently has a foreign friend who writes in oriental calligraphy. Soon I will learn in what part of the city she purchased the Chinese, or India, ink she uses, and therefore where she lives. I *will* find her. Can you imagine the thrill of seeing her as I am looking at you at this moment! My twin sister! Better yet—my double!"

The swimming pool of the Castle, with its naked bodies and dammed-in water—was it the image of water as savage enemy? D— neither disrobed nor bathed:

"We are the way, the truth, and the life . . . we are destined for the agony of the flesh. . . . In twenty-nine minutes the party will begin . . . and we will ascend to the bestial orgasm of the *Ramapithecus punjabicus,* ladies and gentlemen."

D— kissed my forehead and took my left elbow with his right hand:

"A pornographic demon sent me this Fair Maiden. Had I been a virgin I would have received this gift from the hands of an archangel. Had I been the mother of a Buddha, from an elephant."

The water of the pool writhed, wormlike. It did not symbolize plenitude, nor the fluid dynamism of thought, nor fertility.

"We have but a few moments to wait, your reverences. I will present to you cybernetic dogmas full of truths of life eternal. Meanwhile imagine that I am painting with my drooling brushes your testicles or the interior of your vaginal lips."

In the greenhouse water symbolized life. The little channels it took figured forth a model of slow subconscious thought. Water sprinkled the gardens of altruism, made plants grow, soothed insects' thirst, transported splinters. Each droplet was a locus of microscopic life, with millions of living creatures the eyes-of-my-body could not see. It held wetness, tangible humidity in a sphere, the round secret of punctual, certain eternity.

Behind the sentry pathways and the moats, the mobs were less angry than those formed into tight groups about the gate and the watchtower. Were some intoning a hymn? Was desire diluting into song? Was it a kind of hybrid way of participating in the ceremony? Did melancholy compensate for absence?

Moments before the party began, among the guests there started springing up a kind of collective abandon. As a consequence of sexual promiscuity? Did it incite to still other abandons? To those acts most in keeping with the guests' recognition of their own personalities? It appeared that D— desired above all else the celebration of a chain of transient, ritual marriages in the cellar of his Castle:

"A historian of primitive peoples has written that a king obliged all his daughters to prostitute themselves once in their lives. Tonight all of us will be daughters of the king, ladies and gentlemen."

Was depersonalized pleasure to be trumpetted as the vehicle for traversing the frontiers of knowledge?

When K— saw me with my shaven head, moments before I took the train to go to the Castle, he looked upward at the sky for some time:

"What is scorned I honour. The black becomes white and the white, black."

For K— our conduct could be interpreted as deeds of fate. Therefore it was spread all across the sky, like the restive murmur of random chance.

A thin stream of water was leaking from the swimming pool in the Castle. The naked bodies swam on. The little puddle it made, with its slow, measured, ordered revolutions, led me to meditate.

Had K— been an epic he would have recounted the life of the world's first women living among wild beasts and domesticated creatures. Had he been a *Bildungsroman* he would have described the woman who transfigured her blood into meaningful ideas. Had he been a history textbook he would have related the transubstantiation of the energy in stars. Had he been a treatise in philosophy he would have taught, organized, and guided the evolution of the intelligence with all its vicissitudes, its rises, and its falls. Had he been a science book he would have analysed the regions of light and the meanderings of shade of the *Ding an sich.* Had he been a novel the heroine, by caprice or by fatality, would have descended into the realm where one is blinded by excess of light. Had he been a poem, he would have crossed seven bridges on which his ornaments would have been stripped from him and he would have been invested with the power to communicate the grace which floods him.

Did strength lodge invisible in his dreams?

LADIES AND GENTLEMEN! LET THE festivities begin! The single yet absolutely stringent and emblematic rule demands that for the duration of the evening no one refuse any devotion paid thighs, loins, or belly by the stranger who desires one. Our ungated orifices may be penetrated without warning. Our evening's destiny is to vibrate, tremble, quiver, and enjoy. We shall be horses with mares, mares with studs in heat, studs corralled with studs, mares in uterine flame for one another."

The guests sat along the tiers of an amphitheatre. The stage was a dais upholstered with a Persian carpet:

"We will give in to inhuman temptation, we will stoke it most brutally or most delicately. We will break away from the social customs of respect and esteem for our fellow creatures, from social politeness. Only the compass needle of pleasure will guide us. We will wallow in humiliation and vice so as to arrive at last at unnatural delirium. The only thing which can justly and coherently be compared with our becursed natures is infamy itself! And now, to begin, a little dish to whet your appetites!"

Two naked women caressed one another on the stage. With whips. Were they whipping each other, really? Were the lashes simulated? D— contemplated the scene from his perch on the right edge of the dais. He asked them to penetrate each other with the handles.

Human episodes boiled with anxiety and restlessness. Two

or three hours before the party was to begin, S—'s impatience changed to resignation:

"One legend tells that a certain courtesan cried each day until her robes were completely soaked with tears. She wanted to be the Prince's favourite. When at last she reached her goal and was installed in the palace, and was eating the most exquisite of dishes, she asked herself whether she had not been crying in her sleep and on awakening had not realised that life is a dream."

When the two women kissed on the stage the Castle's guests could not conceal their disappointment. D— aimed his pointed tongue at them. At the perineal folds of one of them?

S— was absorbed in their tumult:

"You know how impatiently I have waited for this party, how carefully I have prepared you for it . . . but it will be in vain. The most voracious appetites, the tastes D— calls the most depraved cannot be conceived of as a priestly calling because they are only *symptoms* of the malady, of vertigo, of submission, of debility. And yet I am still as excited as though I were awaiting the arrival of fecundity itself. In certain tribes, the holy man, or shaman, sodomizes his son to fertilize the land. That reminds me of a feminine paradigm, probably utopian, but which enchants me—the woman who loves tenderly, without pleasure, at the same time as she takes her pleasure with hostility."

D— asked his guests to take the stage and tell, in detail, about their vices, their fantasies, their pornographic dreams, and that they act out on the dais a brief scene summarizing their relationships with their companions:

"We will be the *voyeurs* of our own wantonness."

At times in the Firmament I would contemplate the dust which trembled in a ray of sunlight. An atom of dust could surround me, cover me, enclose me, extend me infinitely, perfect me. It was only a ray of sun which passed . . . which was passing as splendid, unique, infinite, and empty as space and its astonishing reflexions.

The Captive and the Marquis, on the little stage of the amphitheatre, once again told their fable. When she repeated again the litany of her humiliations, the audience was enthralled. The Marquis asked them to insult her, pummel her, spit on her. The paralytic, after giving her a beating, demanded that she tell what she felt, bound and alone, locked in the crypt, and why she did it.

He forbade her to cry. The Marquis announced that he was going to brand the mark of his coat of arms on her right buttock with the red-hot poker from the fireplace. The Captive confessed that fire terrified her. Nonetheless she said that she would try, for him, to bear up under it, so as to give him all the pleasure he had ever sought. The Marquis ordered that while he was branding her she accept his member in her mouth. Did the Captive, by dint of pain and degradation, achieve the ultimate heights of insensibility? Did she make that leap to the next phase of the visible? Did she take leave of her self, her body, her name? Not, thus, to depend on substance? Once dissolved, did her broken and toppled body, her flesh, her blood, wander aimlessly through a harsh infinity of darkness?

Leaning against the wall, I admired the Castle's greyhound. It was sleeping beside the fireplace, completely removed from the world. Like me? I had dismissed my eyes, my ears, my mouth, my nose. My breathless body stood like some dead tree, like a dead coal. My spirit flew among the clouds— hanging in a gondola from a hot-air balloon? Clutching the wings of a carrier pigeon? As though it would fly to the centuries-old sequoia in the Park?

A smell of scorched flesh and the Captive's screams brought me back. Had the Marquis defiled, debased himself? Had the Captive been humiliated? Was spiritual horror fascinating? Could tenderness spring up in the wake of pleasure? And rise above the cloud and the memory which mimicked absence?

The guests, inflamed by the degradation, were swarming on top of one another. The normal course of their prudence had been deflected. Did they believe that in this way they could reflect the black image of the nature they abhorred?

S—, transfigured by a harsh and violent heat, asked me to tie him to a tiny table set into a niche under the corner stair-tower. His proferred mouth fell to the left while his backside opening was reared to the right. He burned for any passing guest to seize him and possess him. It made him happy to be thrown down on the table in that dark corner like a forgotten wineskin. I bound his hands, his ankles, and his neck with rope and blindfolded his eyes with a scrap of black cloth as he had asked me to do.

When the minnows began to stir up the Vat, the molecules of water seemed to be in a delirium. Were the tiny fish the creators of a simulacrum of chaos? Of a parody of rebellion? Did the minnow incite his fellows to disorder as an imitation of evil for a few brief instants? Could one imagine that in those seconds the minnow was dreaming of engendering pain and death? Did S— wish all the newlyweds to be bound, two by two, and to be thrown thus, trussed together, as though part of the marriage ceremony, into the deepest part of the sea? Did he aspire to be the only surviving witness to that slow submarine agonized sinking into death? To strike the indispensable spark so that the sacrifice would snuff out fate?

As the festival progressed, in the Castle's underground, the participants began naturally dividing into four groups. The Masters, with D— at their head, had as their mission to instruct, propose, order, recite, suggest. The Warriors were in charge of exercising immediate power in the most violent conceivable way. The Serving Class—servants, serfs, slaves, servo-robots—were an obedient, disciplined mass which wholly depended on the desires, whims, caprices, furies, or raptures of the Warriors. The Versatiles might serve or command, according to the demands of the liturgy ordered by the Masters, or to circumstances.

The warriors employed a savage technique of assimilation. The servant, obliged to forgo all his own characteristics, had

to adapt himself to the demands of the warrior whose vassal
he had become, in an unlimited act of submission. During the
period of conquest he would live in accordance with the strict
rules of his subjugator. He abstained from taking any initiative
whatever and meekly accepted any violence. He was being
trained for his future automatic behaviour.

The masters might, paradoxically, act as servants or as warriors, so long as they did not adopt any posture which did not
strictly follow the rules of outward conduct. They acted out
their roles, without feeling.

The beauty, truth, mercy, that lay somewhere between happiness and the earth—did they burst like impossible dreams?

There would be moments when the structure of the groups
at the party was frozen and moments at which it shifted and
changed. Distinctions, *nuances,* could be established within
the groups. Among the serving class, goldworkers and manual
labourers were judged inferior to blacksmiths and enchasers.
Throughout the night hierarchies were built up and refined.
The system was thereby made more repressive and at the same
time more complex.

Among the serfs their origins were taken into account:
What warrior had brought them to the Castle? What stage of
taming had they merited or achieved? What were they capable
of? To what tests had they been submitted?

Warriors sought to bring each servant to his breaking point.
They skimped neither on beatings and mistreatments nor on
verbal abuse and profanations. When they reached that point
of rupture, the other warriors collaborated with the violator
to deepen and widen the victim's fissure. This collaboration
nonetheless left the initiative, the choice of abuse and outrage,
to the warrior who had originally managed to break down the
servant's resistance.

Intergroup relations were marked by violence. All forms of
tenderness, love, or simple affection were tacitly but strictly
forbidden. Warriors only shared drink with their peers. Serfs
were forbidden to drink, under penalty of their warriors' spit-
ting in their mouth. The warriors rigidly ruled every servant's

behaviour, his breathing, the way he looked about or moved his body. When a warrior commanded some attitude of the mouth or abdomen, a certain motion by the hands or tongue, the servant had to perform it perfectly and instantaneously until his conqueror ordered the performance ended. Since the number of serfs and slaves increased as the night wore on, and at the same time since the masters and versatiles ordinarily preferred, when it came to choosing, to obey rather than to command, soon every warrior had a stable of slaves under his dominion.

Within that structure no one was permitted to complain of injustice. Warriors were constantly on guard to see that everyone accepted the norms which prevailed. They demanded that every person recognise that he deserved the place he occupied. They were ever alert to see that this recognition be engraved in the mind of every conquered serf. When a slave licked his warrior's feet he was performing the duties of his estate with the same care, dedication, and concentration as when he painfully received in his bowels the clenched fist of his dominator. On the hierarchical scale, each creature aspired to be treated as an individual belonging to the group in which he had been set.

No one could climb upwards. One could not rise from slave to warrior, nor from warrior to master. The versatiles, after brief experiences as conquerors, descended to the category of servants, there to remain once and for all. When warriors slapped them, they repeated, crestfallen:

"All experience is pain."

Did sufferings flow like veins in search of other veins? To lose themselves in some clogged swamp?

Warriors, as the night advanced, multiplied their demands. The physical suffering they caused their servitors seemed to them illusory payment. They constantly needed more and more. In parallel, servants seemed to find in pain and outrage the ecstasy of their self-renunciation. It was said that in the most burning of their pleas they might achieve for a brief instant the fulfilment of their instinct's needs. This state could only be reached, it was confusedly claimed to have been proved, by way of the torments inflicted on them by their owners. The fury of the warriors was fed by the self-evident fact that they, on the other hand, were unable to achieve such a revelation of their own. As time passed, warriors and slaves needed ever more fury, heat, and violence, for motives paradoxically parallel and contradictory.

The self-renunciation of the servants was considered a radical and irreversible rupture. The immediate, painful consequences were obvious. But the slaves discovered in this break a path theretofore unknown whose final destination was likewise a mystery to them. They were at the mercy of the unrestrained act of a warrior to be conducted to the apotheosis of suffering, to death.

The spectacle of slaves who had agreed to renounce life engendered anger and vengefulness among the warriors. The other slaves, who had not yet reached that height, contemplated them with disgust. Were they attempting to defend themselves in this way against an action which they envied and which yet endangered not only their dignity and their happiness, which they had already given over to their warriors, but also even their lives?

The slave who renounced himself was forced to declare the fact publicly—he was stripped of his soul before the wrath of the entire congregation. From that moment on, he could not turn his glance on the warriors. He became a corpse. His warrior could only communicate with him by way of kicks which were to be always rightly interpreted. They tirelessly strayed through the underground. They knew they had to abandon all hope of ever being killed by their conquerors.

Did they lay down all emotion on the verge of a chasm opening onto rot and bedlamite confusion?

S— had shaved my head for the second time a few hours before the party began:

"D— has a frenzied worship of orgasm—as though it were original light. It is a man's, a *macho*'s passion, which I will never know. . . . He no doubt wants the absolute crime to be committed sometime during the night . . . but as it only exists in his imagination. . . . He will have a *simulacrum* performed . . . or if not that, he will dream of it aloud."

As he passed the electric razor over my head I was reminded of K—:

"One can float without knowing how to swim, walk through fire without being burned, fall into space without breaking a single bone. Without artifice, without fear . . . simply by inhaling and exhaling with purity."

THROUGHOUT OUR RETURN TRIP, S—
kept looking at my wig. He had settled it on my shaved
head once the party had ended. To blot it out? He also took
all the paint off my face. So that every vestige of the event
should be erased?

The syncopated cadence of the wheels of the train—did it
keep rhythm with the pulse of my blood? With the natural heat
of desire? With existence, which in a trice drowned me? I
looked over at S—, sitting facing me in the compartment. I
recalled him in the bathtub in the dungeon, complying with,
keeping the obligations which his servitor's role imposed on
him. Why did he take no pity on his body? Did he consider
it a great feat to be urinated on, chained down by the warriors?

During the party had decomposition and debasement been
admired as perfect works of nature? Did pleasure in degrading
another reveal itself to be an instinct now codified? Could it
slip into a magical phase? Fantastical? *Passionnelle?* Like a *lon-
gueur* horrifyingly tied to suffering and anguish?

The evening's frenzy had been unloosed through the Castle
in three stages. In the first stage, the serving class's acts of
self-humiliation and self-surrender might be compared to
those subterfuges which, according to one or another legend,
certain women in the past would use to sate their lusts without
losing their honour. In the second phase, the servant's recompense was his fervent faithfulness. In the third, the warrior
would put his servant to the test, to determine whether his
submission was corporeal or of the consciousness. Subjugation

was transformed into the carnal instrument of pleasure. The warrior would require his servant to obey not out of passion, nor from any personal attraction or power which the master might exert on him, but rather out of the complete destruction of the serf's personality.

D— did not hesitate a second before that brazen act:

"Ladies and gentlemen, sexuality beyond bounds, like the First-Class sections of trains, is monopolized by spirits either emancipated or of divinely inspired genius. Five centuries ago a religious prince, during a festive occasion such as this one, ordered fifty courtesans stripped nude. He had them on all fours pick up chestnuts his attendants flung before them on the floor. Afterward the prince proportioned gifts to his guests who had publicly offered the greatest proofs of virility. Four centuries ago the freest women of the aristocracy allowed themselves to be raped by gangs of young men in the woods which surrounded the great cities. Tonight a deluge of vice and depravity will reach heights never achieved before—we will prefigure the End of the World."

One couple arrived at the party very late. When they passed through the observation tower and stood at the brink of the sunken floor where the events of the evening had already begun, they recoiled a step in horror. The spectacle was not that which they had expected. Two warriors broke into rude derisory laughter.

"So you thought you had been invited to an exhibit of *risqué* painting! Your lordship, here there is no painting, but rather the reality. You, my lady, are surrounded by depraved beings ready to explore and exploit the weaknesses of a well-brought-up *ingénue* like yourself. We have been awaiting the Faithful Wife. I can hardly suppose that you will commit the low vulgarity of being shocked and turning tail and running with your husband. . . . Excellent! . . . I suggest, then, to begin, that your spouse and I undress you and deliver you over to these warriors so that they can tame you."

The incredulous Wife—did she enjoy this? Did she think she was in attendance at a theatrical performance? Her husband looked hypnotised. Was it out of defiance that they at first accepted, agreed to the postures demanded of them? Were they at every moment expecting rescue, after the first fog of lust and submission had been burned away?

The train went on toward the Firmament, and I asked myself whether K— would be waiting for me on the station platform.

The two warriors systematically explored the Wife's body, with the object of finding the posture which was most becoming to her. They taught her the discipline of the hands, of the mouth, of the feet, and, at last, of the breathing. When this stage began the Wife turned her head toward her husband. Did she want to ask him to come to her aid? Her husband stepped back, his eyes bulging, as though he would have melted away into the wall. No one could help her. Was she gradually losing her ability to think, to reason, to make decisions? The warriors imposed on her a stringent rhythm of respiration—from time to time they halted it, from time to time they made it race. At last they had come to control her.

"Observe, ladies and gentlemen, how the Wife has been transformed into a mare, a ewe. The warriors have laid the yoke upon her, have made her accept it and pull the cart with all her strength. Sir knight, behold how your spouse has been subjected to the will of these two warriors. Observe how they control her movements, her breathing, her very will. Her appetites, especially those which you know nothing of after all these years of marriage, her every concupiscent thought and urge, her aggressivity, her devotion, all her senses, have been broken, mastered by this brace of warriors, and in your very presence, sire. . . . They have brought your wife around to their designs. Now, if you called her, she would not hear. She is dominated by the brute force of her conquerors. They have obliged her to bend her body and her mind, so that the two parts, together, may advance into a region utterly repugnant to her. Contemplate her, reborn, transformed into a disciplined mare, a female beast of burden, ready to carry, or be mounted by, the first Vandal who passes by."

Why did the husband weep? Was he weighed upon by a bitter, confused awakening, by revelations come too late?

"These warriors, sir knight, have not subjugated your wife for the sole pleasure of constraining her. They demand of her, as you can see for yourself, that she forget her old ways of thinking, walking, breathing, desiring. She has adopted the ways of doing those things that have been conceived and imposed by her conquerors. The discipline of her loins, of her mouth, of her hands, has allowed her spirit to be raped."

Why did her husband go on crying? Why was he beating himself with a flat wooden plank? When D— stopped addressing him, no one paid any more attention to him. The Wife and the two warriors—did they forget that he had collapsed at the foot of the buttress jutting from the wall?

Had the Faithful Wife disengaged herself, or been disengaged, from the outside world?

On occasion in the Firmament the tortoise withdrew inside itself, hiding feet and head under its carapace. Was that its way of fleeing the Firmament? Had the Wife, led by the warriors, found a way to disconnect her brain from the messages, the impulses which otherwise would have brought loud and scandalized reactions from her? Was she now defenceless? Had she discovered, nonetheless, an inward universe thitherto unknown? Did she perceive the phantoms of that universe as the more abject, the better to sate herself with them? Did the taming demand that all the force of her spirit be concentrated in the will to surrender herself, and in the vilest and most degraded way? Did the warriors thereby find the way utterly and completely to dominate her passions and her external and internal organs?

How many *chimeras* lurked, forever chained, behind a single *chimera?* How many monstrosities mired in capricious labyrinths and mazes! What a tiny shrunken fable locked in lackluster (black and lightless) chaos!

When D— bade us goodbye, was there any necessity to venerate him? Why did he strike me as K—'s twin brother?

"Only consider, Fair Maiden, that last night, with the aid of your immaculate mediation, I lived through my second honey-moon. That unforgettable first one, provided me by my infi-nitely beloved wife, occurred precisely forty-six years ago today. Only with an angel could more idyllic relations be imagined than those I shared with you last night. You some-how divined without knowing it that a drop of my sperm is worth ingots of gold. Thanks to your bold skills as a mediaeval Fair Maiden, I was transfigured into the Hero when I asked you to martyrize me. You performed that act with such faith and such mercifulness—would you have been capable of kill-ing me, sweet Fair Maiden, had I asked it of you? . . . I feel spasms in my very bowels when I remember your serene sternness. The North Wind which blows through this realm communes with my memories. I will relive in these next few nights, oneirically, platonically, paradisally, the memory of those supplications to which with such refinement you acceded throughout the night. My equilibrium needed this emotional buffeting and upheaval.''

Was life, for the insects of the Firmament, a chain of imme-diate necessities? What place did the appetite for food occupy in that chain? What place the cosmic obligation to procreate? Did translucent naughts imprison the string of rosary-beads of fatality in a nothingness without exit or return?

When I returned to the Keep I immediately noted the grow-ing disorder which the Maimed One's turmoil geographically spread:

"The circle is narrowing! I hear the decadence, as though it were a horse behind a curtain of fog, galloping closer and closer! And this is the moment you choose to go off God knows where! Can you not see how the very foundations beneath us are crumbling! . . . Who will spill a single nostalgic tear over us? . . .''

The Sisters put new lightbulbs in the lamps and lanterns of the Keep. In the shadows of the huge empty *salons* and long hallways ghastly lights dangled and danced from rusty, cob-webbed, motheaten cords. Packages, trunks, luggage, heaped-up household implements—did they give form to lurking terror? Were they hulking frightened masses? Defensive? The Sisters, under the Maimed One's command, had jumbled everything together into great piles. To block the advance of decadence? To, cathartically, protect themselves? To eclipse that encroaching rebel light which would drive away the shadows?

"What were you doing away for so long? You have almost come too late to run away with us."

The Maimed One and the Sisters kept themselves locked up before the television screen, awaiting the demise of Him. When it occurred they were ready to leap into the car and drive madly for the frontier. Were they taking the roles of three comedians playing a caricatured family farce? Three gravediggers at a wake in the light of a winking neon sign? Three conspirators stabbing the dead man at a burial?

"The car is in the garage. We have enough petrol to take us far past the border. There is a seat left for you. You must, must come. They are capable of doing the worst thing imaginable to you, just for being your father's daughter."

Was He, for the Maimed One, even before He stiffened in His last agony, transfigured into pure Illusion? Were there any circumstances, or any locations, in which the contraries above and beyond any dualism could be resolved?

"For some time I have been toying with the idea of smoking a peacepipe with them, of joining their cause . . . if only to survive."

The Keep without its furnishings had the aspect of a body with its entrails sucked out. Its household *accoutrements* were piled at the door to the Garden—uniforms, the cabin trunks full of books, briefcases filled with jewellery and loose gems, steamer trunks with tableware, silver, china, tablecloths, hatboxes crammed with scarves and kerchiefs, handkerchiefs, ascots, coffee services, *samovars*. The Maimed One was carrying off the Keep's placental womb with him. So as not to forget?:

"When the time comes for the looting and pillaging . . . they will steal nothing essential."

The garage had become a darkened temple. The Maimed

One and the Sisters visited it often. Did they adore it as the lair of some cult? As the black wreath laid to a distant memory-less paradise?

"The masses sit as though in the audience at His death, not realising that civilisation dies with Him. The very air we breathe is stupid! We are so wretched!"

The life of the Maimed One and the Sisters was shrunk to a shared fear and the bustle of readying for flight. Wide-eyed terror, animal panic, left them with no forms, no names—dispossessed. Was it that inability to have, possess, order, dispose, control that so tortured them and deprived them of all hope?

Trash piled up in the dining room. Papers which were to be destroyed had been swept—by the wind?—into heaps in the study, and furniture was jumbled into crazy stacks in the Fountain in the Garden.

"Everything will have to be burned, so that nothing will fall into the hands of the Huns."

Void, out of pure wild madness, had become plenitude for the three of them. The Keep no longer constituted a refuge, a home, or a residence—only a rootless emptiness. The three creatures wanted to disappear. Not to act? Not to exist? Like the Captive?

The Captive, once during the night in the Castle, took the initiative of rubbing her lips against mine. The Marquis seemed surprised by that spontaneous gesture. As she brushed my mouth with hers I looked into her eyes. Did she undertake by her own means that straight route which would lead her, irremediably, to solitude? Did she set an impassable barrier around herself, so as to feel the pleasure of utter self-confinement? Had she chosen the Marquis and designed the programme, the terms of dependency which most suited her?

"I disgust you!"

Imprisoned, with no other contact with the world than those acts of devotion which the Marquis imposed upon her, the Captive dreamt of a walled-in life, like that the eremites had lived eight hundred years before the Firmament. She longed to sit in her cell, huddled as though in a dungeon, with no window but a chink to admit air. To receive each day the minimum ration necessary to stave off starvation or thirst. Did the bottomless darkness from which emerged a confusion of fierce shadows hold the blinding light which would reveal the simple elements of her universe?

The Captive looked at the eyes-of-my-body. Did she dream of a Soirée? I had travelled to the Castle without P—'s razor.

"Would you like to kill me? Slit my throat with a razor? Do I disgust you? . . . I nauseate myself! . . . The spectacle of my corruption reflects that of the very world itself. . . . Wouldn't you like to slit my throat? Cut off my head! You find me sickening, don't you?"

With her tongue she poked at the tongue-of-my-body.

"Tell me I am filth and offal! Say it!"

Did the Captive find her way through the maze of her body by the grace of knots of energy? Why would she want once and for all to close herself up in darkness? As though in a tomb? Could she, thus entombed, become one with eternal silence? Meditate over breath as the basis of Word? Most especially over what in our bodies tends downward with our excrement? Over the all-levelling fire? Was it thus that the Captive could hear her own pulse, her own throbbings? Dissect the circulation of her blood through the particles of her body? Did she dream of centuries of solitude and silence? Of a sweet sempiternal amnesia into which her weary soul would plunge, as into glowing brilliance?

When I saw K— again, he was meditating, motionlessly, even when he spoke to me under the centuries-old sequoia:

"The body is sacred . . . emanates from and is a reflexion of the universe . . . participates directly and spontaneously in its essence."

The first rays of the morning sun filtered through the branches of the sequoia. Like glittering omens. They floated and hovered over K—'s body as though in obedience to its desires.

THE POLICE FINALLY KNOW WHAT neighbourhood the murderess lives in. They came across the stationer's where she buys her India ink. And they are beginning to show a bit of interest in the cameo she had pinned to her blouse when she killed the man in the Cinema. The waiter in the Bar described the carving on the gemstone of the brooch. He said he believed it was antique. How did the murderess come to own it?"

The Keep was the foundation of a City-State where private property was unknown. The Maimed One was the custodian of a theocratic monarchy: he governed the territory and administered the law.

During eras of radical heterodoxy, the sky's role was supposedly that of the male; the earth's, the female. They came together to procreate, and the elements were their offspring. These in their turn made possible life in the greenhouse and the universe outside its walls. The firstborn of their union was air. Its progenitors wanted to have it all to themselves—the sky, to be carried by it ever higher, and the earth, simply to hold it and participate thereby in its fertility. Of those conflicts and squabbles there still remain such vestiges as tempests and cyclones. Water believed it had spontaneously sprung from the earth, by parthenogenesis. Therefore, the wisest and most prudent species of ants fertilized their eggs themselves, without the aid of males, in nests in which only females had existed for century upon century.

Oh luxuriance of branches branching unattainable!

The sweet water spread throughout the universe, creating rivers, springs, lakes, creeks, torrents. Graciously obeying the universal order made it eligible for incalculable benefits, according to these heterodox hypotheses. The Sisters also upheld this proposition, until His long death-agony plunged the Maimed One's idealism into frenzy:

"In a situation of moral collapse such as the one we find ourselves in now, everything we know serves for nothing. Before us is rearing a force which is irrational, savage, virtually bestial."

The abundance which had before been enjoyed had come from the system—and from the sky. So proclaimed the three inhabitants: all known geography benefitted from the winds of wealth. Obedience to law transformed the Keep into an impregnable bastion, multiplied products in shops, filled barns and granaries, loaded the shelves and bins of warehouses. Wealth even, according to the Maimed One, entered the most modest little notions shop or mud-walled den. A perdurable peace quietly reigned in the very fact that Things Existed:

"We have lived through, without really becoming aware of it, glorious, jubilant decades. Even the inferior orders of men, in those shining years we have just enjoyed, were cousins, albeit distant ones, in the great family of man."

The Keep had gone through a legendary era during which labourers did their work and received their share of the gain. *Haciendas,* farms, lovely gardens, kitchen plots were tilled, while at the same time homage was rendered to the tutelary Lord. There would pass long times, so the Maimed One recalled, during which the feast of union, harmony, and prosperity would be celebrated with great rejoicing and amidst terrible hostility to the incubus and obedience to grace.

"They are going to destroy everything. They are going to exterminate all their betters. They will wreak fierce vengeance against us in order to right, or mitigate, the worst of all wrongs—imagined wrongs."

In the Keep, the Maimed One enjoyed certain privileges, to offset the dangers he had faced when he had gone against the darkest powers. The Sisters attended his feasts and participated in the rites, though solely as officiators:

"These barbarians will judge and condemn us, and, like the Emperor who appointed his horse senator, they will be perfectly capable of condemning the Keep too, because it sheltered us."

S— after our return disappeared:

"I did not know—how shall I say this?—I am retrospectively embarrassed and ashamed at what I did in the Castle. Even though you were so calm and contained. . . . Did I shock you? You only looked in my eyes for a moment, when I was in the bathtub. . . . While you were martyrizing D—, I was the one looking at you. You were ready to . . . kill him? And yet it looked as though you admired him so! Did you consider us a gang of perverts and depraved madmen?"

One schism in the Firmament associated knowledge and understanding with excrement, light with shadow, onanism and depravity with fertility. It asserted that as a consequence of these junctions rivers did not dry up, plants ripened, the sun shone, and trees grew.

S— wore the outward trappings of a pervert. As a bird seeks refuge in the nest? Was he confessing to himself, but in my presence? Did his rational thought thereby subdue the most poetic fringe of his inspiration? Did his consciousness ascend?:

"I don't know why, still again, I portrayed myself that way. The damned lapdog that yaps between my legs . . ."

Did what S— called his Vices throw wide open the half-closed founts of his sensibility? Dismiss the guardians of his most secret emotions? Loose the fragile potencies in which longing quivered?:

"Did I live as intensely as it seemed to me I did? Short, mortal moments . . . Listen to me . . . I would like to cross the river, reach the other shore . . . gain that country from which one cannot return. . . . Would you help me?"

Army-ants—were they seeking immortality? Their incessant, repetitive odyssey—did it nourish their desire for the Epic, the Mythological, the Legendary?

S— came down to earth when he thought of the Soirées:

"They have discovered that the murderess lives right in your neighbourhood. The stationer's where she got her India ink is just a few yards from your house. It could be the one where you buy your notebooks. And the police have discovered some notes the porter at the Conservatory wrote down in an old address-book. My intuition that the poor wretch thought the murderess was in love with him is ratified, do you see, by what he wrote. The police are decided—they will give it their all, now that at last there are so many leads. Your neighbourhood is full of policemen."

The Maimed One was furious:

"There have never been so many police around here! These people are getting ready to join up with the renegades when the situation finally comes undone. And they are occupying this sector because they know that we are all upstanding, well-meaning people from good families here."

Was he hiding in fantasy and delirium?

The Maimed One had instituted a relationship with the Sisters founded on devotion. He accepted their homage after assuming the role of the Sacrificed. He offered a doctrine in which self-surrender and pride merged. As legislator and administrator of the Keep he gave up all that he had. This sacrifice, in spite of the fact that in principle it was a freely given gift, could not go without recompense. The Sisters readied the expiation. They undertook to bathe him with great delicacy and pampering, to carefully clean the foulest orifices of his anatomy, to give him long slow massages, to flush from him, by alcohol rubs and a series of steaming-hot baths, the scum and dregs held in the pores of his body. And as a parallel, by virtue of sacrificing himself, the Maimed One acquired an unvanquishable supremacy over the Sisters:

"They are going to destroy what for so many years I have been building, what I have so laboured at."

The Maimed One told the Sisters that, in the form of protections and ineffable indulgences, he would repay them, infinitely augmented, everything he received from them. They therefore felt themselves obliged to lavish upon him new gifts, delights, and services. And these richnesses in turn brought about the concession of still more benefactions, ever more spiritual. Thus came about a chain which nourished the coherence and the oscillation of the Keep, ever tending toward ruin in chaotic gloom and darkness.

The Maimed One pointed out the inequality of the exchanges. He possessed the incalculable treasure of self-surrender. His sacrifices, even in potentiality, could not be compared with the exclusively physical presents bestowed on him by the Sisters. On occasion the Maimed One would insist upon the laughable nature of the offerings, ablutions, lavings, dishes of food he received from them, in comparison with the exalted magnanimity of his own altruistic beneficences. The Maimed One would make perfectly clear that he was prepared to lay down his very life, while the Sisters only provided services, and would only immolate themselves under the most extraordinary circumstances. The Maimed One, as it behooved him to do, was prodigal with gifts, advice, prizes, punishments, experience, light itself. He was not, moreover, insensible to the fervour with which he was treated. He begged, therefore, that the Sisters crown their every movement with the grace of sincerity, especially during massages, rubdowns, and suctions. There, the time expended lent value to the offering. On occasion the Maimed One would bring his reception of their homage to an end with a carping and unexpected behest:

"Read to me!"

He received the words of the reading as an invocation or a chant. Each phrase read and enunciated aloud by one of the Sisters brought him inestimable delight. He could have spoken volumes on the respective merits of caresses and being read to. Therefore he often had both performed at once. The indissoluble presence of the two elements changed the rendered offerings not into a third which was the sum of the two, but rather into an act utterly other, and superior. Sometimes, as he himself recognised, he stopped listening to the reading, but the mere fact of knowing that one of the Sisters was

moving her lips and eyes gave him a pleasure which bound-
lessly increased the ravishment which the hands of the other
were simultaneously provoking in him. Those hands—were
they landscape? And the voice—atmosphere? And together—
the two addends rife with appearance for a sedentary man
adrift in sense?

What was essential for the Maimed One was that the two
acts, touch and enunciation, partake of the necessary elements
of any offering—intention, devotion, authenticity. "Read just
a bit slower and ever so little louder."

Reading had many points of similarity with food. Obviously
the Maimed One, depending upon his whims or his natural
demands, might consume one or another nutriment. When
they presented it to him, the Sisters held to strict rules. As one
introduced into his mouth, with infinite care, the delicacy, the
other was not to modify in the slightest the motions of her
hands and lips.

"This is all going to go smash. All dignity is lost. Turn on
the television, the programmes are about to start."

Did the television possess hallucinogenic qualities? Did it
operate on its viewers to produce behaviour modification?
From what moment did the Maimed One pay less attention to
the Sisters' offerings and more to the screen? For how long
would offerings and adorations coexist and combine? The
three at last gave themselves up altogether to the charms of the
television set. Was it a substitutive liturgy? Was it one sign
among many of the Keep's decadence, measured by its own
standards?

"We are living through the End of the World. Everything
is topsy-turvy. The moment His death is announced on television, we are off . . . not one minute longer!"

The Maimed One's meals were celebrated with inalterable
ceremonial precision. He would lay his head back against the
cushion which covered the chairback. He would barely open
his mouth to admit the bites of food. He chewed very slowly.
His arms hung heavy at his sides as though they had been
forgotten by his body, and his foot rested on a pillowed stool.

The Sisters at these moments considered the Maimed One a kind of altar which held two sacred flames. One of the Sisters placed the foodstuffs and the beverages, slowly, in his mouth, and then delicately wiped the creases of his lips. To make this process fully comprehensible, the Maimed One explained that this offering of food was a message placed in the flame of the mouth as a kind of solemn invocation. With closed eyes he would move his jaws, a sign that the message was received and transmitted. Throughout these banquets the other Sister, kneeling between his legs, caressing and tonguing him, read the Maimed One's thoughts. She was the *confidante* of his most secret desires, the most faithful interpreter and defender of his appetites, the intermediary for his demands, the intercessor in his frenzies. Without her the food proferred by her sister would have seemed insufficient, or imperfect. Any contact between the two sacred fires was prohibited. Each, mouth and loins, was under the care of one of the two Sisters. The world of Above and that of Below. The Mystery was achieved by the two of them united. Thanks to the ceremony, the Maimed One said, he received strength, life, potency. The nectar which below was at last extracted from him by one of the Sisters the Maimed One called the drink of immortality, the sap of cosmic energy. As proof of his generosity, he bestowed it abundantly. The two Sisters unctuously imbibed it, dividing it drop by drop between themselves. And as they ingested it, they received its portion of grace. Sacrifice and libation, according to the Maimed One, maintained and perpetuated that cycle of dazzling virtues by the grace of which they existed.

Those disgusting bodies, so mismatched, an odd lot, squeezed each other's every square inch.

Was for K—the essential thing to exist like the blink of an eye? And in that terribly short length of time, did he really propose to be happy?

"When I joined the *sumo* stable, I promised to be like the line that runs to the future and, thereby, to live with courage and uprightness."

K— WAS WALKING ALONG BESIDE ME, occupying space in the simplest sense:

"It has been so long since I have seen you! . . . Three years ago, you were absent eight days . . . and they seemed less long than these have. . . . Only when you stay with me can I perfectly integrate myself into all that surrounds me."

Hanging from his shoulders by a little cord K— wore an embroidered scapular. Inside, it held a small shaving of wood with a maxim penned in calligraphy:

"With you I speak not only with my mouth and with my reason, but with my ears and with my eyes. And so, when you were away, I dreamt of you while asleep and dreamily thought of you while awake. I felt you, at a distance, while you were in the Castle, with my muted senses."

What guided the insects of the Firmament in their amorous relations? The spiritual splendour of the other partner? Ought one believe in telepathy?

"The heart is a source of life-illuminating radiations. That is why I can make you out even when you are invisible to my senses. My heart's eye is utterly *clairvoyant!*"

K—, motionless, gazed at me for a long long time. Was he thinking of nothing? His two eyes resting on mine—could they have gone on looking at me, unfaltering? Forever?

"I am possessed of two bodies. But when you are away from me, one of them remains in my studio, on its *tatami* mat, while the other makes its way to you. It is my *envoy.* I see it emerge from my heart and fly. It can spring up spontaneously, or at my will. I glimpse it soaring and then landing where you are—enchanted. These eight days you were at the Castle I spent practising *sumo* and playing the flute. You moved through space while I waited for you. I could not continue to exist without overcoming your absence. I had to try somehow to get myself into that moving-away, and to follow you."

Why was the sensibility of insects that came into the mating time in the greenhouse so receptive to the mating signals or messages from the other? Did they create a new system of values when they began to feel the heat of desire? A system independent of everything they had learned? Were they unique in triumph, basking in that splendour?

K— sketched out a *silhouette* of togetherness:

"When you are with me I feel I achieve the Supreme Good, reach equilibrium. I experience a happiness which purifies passion, transforms it, and checks its violence. I feel the urge to perform the loveliest acts, to be supremely upright, generous, altruistic, virtuous, and capable of love—I feel it, with every breath, filling my brain."

In the greenhouse, those insects which could receive an amorous message at a considerable distance belonged to species which had an extremely short lifespan. On the other hand, those insects which never felt that imperious, exacting call, that irresistible attraction, lived for years—decades—, like the ants, for example.

"I have never felt such melting tenderness. For others, and for myself as well. A tenderness born of love. During your absence I felt love raised to its epitome."

The two cockroaches I was watching in the Firmament were very far away from each other. The male was in the midst of the Steppes of Discourse, while the female was under the foundations of the Temple of Twilight. The male, rutting, secreted a thick liquid from glands in his abdomen. Was it a message he wrote on the ground? The female, seduced, seemed to read it at once—as though it were a suddenly lit neon signboard glowing in the dark. She started off at once, scurrying towards him, unconscious of danger. Did love allow her to forget her head, forget all of herself, her feet, her antennae? The only place in the Firmament that existed for her was next to him. The male cockroach—was he the symbol of perfect happiness? The path to him was long, hard. There was always the possibility that the female might be attacked by predators or higher animals. But was it that she could no longer live without the other? She scuttled across obstacles which looked to be impassable by her clumsy little female cockroach body. Because she *had* to merge with that longed-for image? Had she lost all sense of responsibility? All reason to live as an individual of a species? Was she rushing to ecstasy? Was she, with this suicidal race, negating herself? Or did she expect with it to realise herself in the most perfect way? Such palpably gracious reserve in her backwardness!

Did K— covet absolute light and magnificence?

"Thinking of you I realised that one can renounce love for love's sake. The renunciation is love as well. I had the voluptuous impression that I was becoming you. I perceived you as so different from myself! And at the same time, so alike! You were coming back in the train from the Castle, and I was following you yard by yard—from this distance. I passed through the landscape with you, coming from imagination to reality. We flew through the cosmos. Just when I was about to faint from vertigo I found a spot, a point, a place at which you were you and I, I. You represented absolute refuge to me, the centre of centres."

The palm of K—'s hand swept over my forehead. Then it softly slid down to my throat.

"I caress not your forehead but my inexistence, and that of my predecessors, the men and women who lived among animals two million years ago."

In the midst of his secretions, the male cockroach stands motionless in an attitude of waiting. The female is approaching. When at last she appeared to him on the Steppes of Discourse did he guess, or perceive, that he was no longer drawing his breaths alone? Could he smell the aroma of frenzy spreading headlong into a fugitive—ephemeral?—future?

Was it the fleeting intensity of that moment that seduced K—?

"The inequality between me and you, your superiority, is not the only basis of my admiration for you . . . of my adoration. But it should not be, either, any obstacle to a complete spiritual communion."

While the two cockroaches were still some distance from each other, was the male's desire greater than the female's? More ardent? And during her approach did the female's impatience metamorphose into reproach? Doubt? Melancholy? Pain? Desperation? Did she ever, even for one instant during her reckless and dangerous voyage, imagine that the male had died? Did she need him? Physically? Spiritually? As an individual? As a member of his group? Was she the victim of obsession? Of anti-natural impulse? Of instinct? Was the male everything to her? And she, everything to him? For the entire trip? Beginning at what instant? Could one conceive that the two of them were transported with joy when they met and came together at last?

Was K—'s impatience hastening him on?:

"I need to fuse with you spiritually, join our hearts and understandings."

How many million female cockroaches existed in the Firmament? How many males? What was the calculable mathematical probability that the two cockroaches I had observed would come together? What were the causes of this most improbable union? Why did this and only this female receive the message? How was it destined for her? Did chance determine it? How? My hands, as they built the Firmament—had they from the beginning, from even before the cockroaches' birth, intervened, had some part, in their fates? How? What was it that the male had desired in the female when he had seen her from just inches away, on the Steppes of Discourse? Her whole body? One part of it only? Especially? The way she moved? Was still? Her smell? The almost imperceptible motion of her antennae? Could they realize the interpenetration of their abdomens without the bonds of love? In that case, did the union signify a regression? A victory? How was respect expressed between two cockroaches? Would the male have enjoyed the troubled intensity of a rape? Could there exist a pleasure brought on by the physical rapture of the other? Like that of the sheep in the fable of the Church kowtowing not to the Rock itself but rather to the Word?

K— continually wooed an inexhaustible truth:

"While I was waiting it came to me—like a revelation—that it is you who have bound me to love. You chose me, three years ago, when I arrived here to spend ten days in this city from which today I would not stir an inch. You conquered me. And conquered too, unknowingly, my *sumo* master. Otherwise he would never have ordered me to make the journey. Chance is the key to gambling and to fascination as well. My master was my spiritual father—love and sternness. The stable was my home. I lived in it with my spiritual brothers, the other *sumo* wrestlers. We ate together from the common bowl, we slept in the same room, we trained on the same mat. We were going to be famous, and rich, as *sumo* wrestlers, but we were never to abandon that stable, nor our family, nor our master. . . . Yet he sent me here—to meet you! He knew I would abandon my sport, my art, that I would lay my life's principles at your heart and that from your heart I would receive the only aid that might keep me from death or self-destruction. Your hand guides me. And he knew it. That is why he told me nothing. The master neither teaches nor counsels, he only *is*—example and firm uprightness."

When the female cockroach reached the male, she licked at the pool of his secretions. Were they amorous distillates? Did that tender gesture symbolize the exchange of blood? Was the female delaying that moment when she would voluntarily fall into another world? Were they sharing moments of frustration? Enjoying expectations by contrariety? Had they planned this delay? Was it a necessary stage? A prologue? An overture? Foreplay? Was the male cockroach imagining, pretending that she was still rushing, and she, that he was still waiting? Could they feel desire grow ever stronger? Could they sense it would devour them? Were they savouring those preludes? That concentrated scent—did it unexpectedly strike them, like some essence which unseats reason and shifts the very foundations of things?

S— would have liked his heart literally eaten:

"When I was a boy I exchanged blood with my friends. We would prick our fingers. I met a man who believed that if you pricked your ring finger and let a few drops of blood fall into your companion's glass of wine, your companion's heart would grow drunken. He called that prick of the finger heart's-mouth."

Was love for K— a promise of immortality?:

"I would like to be inside your heart. Be locked inside your breast. I would like you to be the life of my life. Have endless union. I put aside love's desire, I repress it, mould it. I do not stamp it out. . . . I look after it and keep watch over it. I practise continence while you feed my desire. This harsh abstinence illuminates my chastity and opens the way to all forms of spiritual delight. It also has a sensual character. It is the spring-force of *clairvoyance* and ecstasy—and, indirectly, of lust. You purify my instincts and guide my spirit. Therefore my love has its deepest roots in your body. My chastity is subordinate to my consciousness of what my delight in you would be."

The two cockroaches caressed each other with their antennae. With their eyes but a fraction of an inch apart, they gazed at each other. Did their antennae communicate the vibrations of their abdomens? Were they mutually enchanted? Was the other insect that only one in the greenhouse? The most wonderful living being ever seen? How many pairs of cockroaches before this one had repeated the selfsame acts and motions? And yet why did they live this moment as though it were the only one? Were they dreaming? Did they transform the awareness of the desire inflaming their bodies into impetus, and the impetus into awareness, and so on, in an infinite concatenation?

K— threw himself into a union without parts, without beginning or end, without edge or angle:

"I live between two times—the time of your presence and the time of your absence, between jubilation and suspended animation. My elders taught me to conceal my emotions. I break into new dimensions when I crack the ice of my education and dive into love."

The male cockroach lifted his wings and exposed the glands closest to his waist. Was he undressing? Did the female see this pose as the male's need to identify himself? The male lowered his eyes and proffered his abdomen and back. Was he in effect saying, "I am female"? "To attract you, I will feminize myself"? Did the female cockroach climb atop the male to masculinize herself for love? She put her feet on her partner's abdomen and buried her head in the crease formed by his wings and back. They inversely imitated the posture of a copulating pair. For several moments, she atop him, both immobile—did they love each other? Did they exchange roles to show how fragile and imperfect each was before the other? Were they living moments of union unlimited yet awkward? A *simulacrum*? An inverted betrothal?

K— maintained harmony with his reigning humour:

"The only thing that would truly make me suffer without hope would be the impossibility of proving my love for you. I feel all the tribulations of the flesh when I look at you. The abjectness they plunge me into would blemish me . . ."

K— gazed at me interminably. Was he abandoning himself to a *chimera*? Did he imagine himself a sequoia? An indifferent tree? Beautiful because I too looked at him?:

"I want you to come with me. I want the two of us, together, to be like peripatetic monks. I want to wander the world with you."

K— looked at me, every second more withdrawn into himself, as though more deeply living every moment:

"Will you? . . . You will! . . . Well then? . . . You'll come with me!"

The two cockroaches in the Firmament, after having played the opposite sex's role for a while, entered the final stage. The male stretched his abdomen, contorted it, and plunged it into the female's. Immediately upon doing this, with a brusque flick of his hind parts he twisted her to the ground. The two insects remained linked at their lower abdomens as though they had been leeches. Their heads, pointed in diametrically opposite directions as the two cockroaches coupled—were they gazing at nothingness? Into space? Into infinity? Were their abdomens merged with instinct?, while their heads, with their erect antennae, dreamt? Could their heads have replaced the amorous structures? If they could have spoken would they have said, "I don't want to see it"? Did they symbolize two lucid, and clear, witnesses to a few frantic moments and then an inexorable fate? The two cockroaches—could they now only fall in love with the absence of life? Could only death happily and fully crown that embrace of hind parts? The love they lived through in those instants preceding penetration— was it now nothing but ungraspable nostalgia? Melancholy for a light once and for all time snuffed? Tied together by their entrails, did the two cockroaches now come to know the essence of the ephemeral? Frenzy going Nowhere, frenzy as Means leading to no End, nipped as it were in the bud. Were the motions of their rear parts the spasms of death-agony? Did they have some premonition that every dance ended in blood? Did they know that giving life was calling forth death?

K— made plans for our journey, mapped the itinerary which would take us far far away:

"To the last dwellings of man—which are castles which are huts of spirituality . . ."

The cockroaches' bodies quivered. If I had cut off their heads they would have gone on, decapitated, carrying out instinct's bidding, keeping the repugnant rhythm of the universe outside the walls.

WHEN I ARRIVED AT THE KEEP, the Sisters had long ropes with which they were lashing the last bags to the baggage-rack on the car. They were cramming them into the interstices of the jumbled mass of trunks and boxes. The Maimed One was overseeing the work. He had become the very spit and image of resignation. He had lost the terror which had paralysed him for the last few weeks. And the frantic hyperactivity. He now looked confused, befuddled, dismayed, humbled, and weakened:

"He has died. You must come with us. When all is said and done, you are my daughter. Don't be so obstinate about staying here. We will be off within the quarter hour."

I could sense K— in his studio as though seeing him with my own eyes—he had smoothed out his great kerchief and was putting together the haversack for our journey.

The Sisters looked even more exhausted than the Maimed One. Did they fear losing their roots? Disintegrating? The three of them would escape—the visible was born from that which had no form, and the invisible, from panic. The threat, for them, was more horrifying than its carrying-out could have been. Did they want, under the pretext of confusing fear and terror with vengeance and reprisal, to return to the beginnings, when possessions were unknown? They were fleeing the country, once and for all cutting themselves off from the land which had given them life—because in their eyes it had been transmogrified? Into an ogre? They were abandoning its spontaneity, their legacy. Undertaking a voyage into exile. To transplant themselves? They were returning to the centre of the earth aboard a car-mole-snailshell-kangaroo-tortoise-pupa. Taking the road of desperation without border or end? To pull themselves into it, under its cover, and give up and die? Or to emerge again reborn? Did air itself weigh on them as though their very natures were turning on them, attacking them, from their most secret essences?

K— opened the door of his studio to leave, crossed it, and closed it behind him for ever. Although he was half a mile from me I could hear his breath as though it were softly hissing in my ear.

In the empty Keep, the television still played on. It was the only vestige of his life the Maimed One had left in the dwelling. His will and testament? The screen seemed ensconced in desolation—its monotone message, like a metallized ghost's. It emitted a muted unvarying murmur. Did it look like the intestine down which contractions would never pass again? It showed at last that its variety had been all illusion. The television set had never been a heart. Nor the seat of the moral or intelligent faculties. It had been transmuted into an inanimate, deanimated, soulless motor, but which was capable of neither silence nor repose. It sighed and breathed eternally—endless dissonance, unconsciousness, disharmony. The energy which still flickered on its screen was not light from the sky, nor from the spirit. It had reigned like the sovereign of contemplation, which was inaction. The Maimed One and the Sisters had venerated the machine as though it sat at the centre of an empire from which passions, cupidities, influences rayed out to the farthest boundaries. Its luminous quadrangle broadcast catalepsy. On the screen one saw, at last, an everlasting, inglorious snowfall falling without snowflakes, not over the land, not from the sky, a snowfall without morning or night, colour, or inspiration. It was a quivering dust storm of blinding density. An echoing luminous witness. A relic and a reminder, the infinite bombardment of the void.

In the Fountain in the Garden, heaped atop sticks of wood, all the Keep's contents were piled into a gigantic pyre.

So far as the Maimed One was concerned, everything had already been consumed:

"You will regret not coming with us. . . . But at any rate, as soon as the barbarians attack the house, set the furniture afire. Leave nothing for them to take!"

Everything in the Keep that had been used as a container, or to cook in, or sit on, or snuggle into, or sleep on, had been jettisoned and scorned, rejected flatly and finally by the Maimed One and the Sisters. All those appliances, the objects which one would have thought had been integral parts of the organic fabric of the rooms—everything had been converted into kindling for this funerary pyre. It was made up of a *suite* of objects which once had stood as symbols of the internal harmony of the Keep, transformed now equally into symbols of rupture, isolation, and meaninglessness. The Maimed One had sat in judgement on it all, and sentenced it to burning.

K— walked down the stairs from his studio. He was coming for me—I could feel his fevered pulse even in spite of the distance.

The Garden was completely ravaged, disshevelled, as though the Maimed One and the Sisters had wanted to trample on everything glowing and bright, superlative, everything which had obeyed the Natural Law, which in the past the Garden had enclosed and represented. For years it had been the incarnation of peace, calm, heroism. The seasons had succeeded one another, preparing in the depths of the earth the sudden burst of colour and fertility. Thousands of shapes gave colour, outline, and grace to the immeasurably lovely variety of nature. The Garden had been the antechamber of the Firmament. Now strewn with rubbish, filled with grimy papers, trash, and refuse, it had become the image of desolation and abandonment.

K— was coming towards the Keep. I recalled how he had served me that last cup of tea, in the studio:

"I am getting ready, and I will come for you. I will be at your house within two hours, at the latest. We will set out at once, and we will only take the essential with us in the bundle."

What did K— mean by "the essential"?

"You and I together! We will let ourselves be carried on our voyage by the breath of the universe. We will cross mountains and gorges, days and nights, light and darkness. We will be an intimate part of the heights of heaven and the depths of the earth. We cannot now imagine the incomparable. What does the mayfly, which lives for one morning only, know of evening and night? Cicadas, which live only one summer—can they imagine the winter? And the frog, which lives in its pond—can it envision the ocean? What does the man who has never loved know of its infinitudes? What does he know of mysteries if he is surrounded by custom?"

I crossed the Garden and entered the greenhouse. The bubbles in the Vat were boiling and sputtering. S— was sitting on the straw mat waiting for me. Around him spread the sanctuaries, pyramids, the monuments of the Firmament, the Train halted at the foot of the Vigorous Mountains. S—'s presence shattered the peace and order of the Firmament's eyes, ears, nose, mind, and intelligence. What S— knew, or thought he knew, could not be fitted into the providence of the Firmament.

"You will have to forgive me. . . . I could not waste a single minute more. . . . I had to see you . . . at once. Your father and your aunts were most kind to me, . . . they offered to let me wait for you here. They said it was your retreat. . . . I came up the ladder . . . and here I am, you see, quite impatiently waiting for you. The police are about to discover the murderess. . . . The commissioner leading the investigation told me it was only a matter of a few hours now. I called him on the telephone. I passed myself off as the private secretary of the Minister of the Interior. He fell for the ruse, he told me everything about the investigation, the clews, the search—and he told me they had a plan to arrest her, by surprise. . . . I too know who the murderess is."

K— was now hastening toward the Mansion. He was but a score or fewer yards away. I could sense his desire, his longing, his belly swaying along the avenue, his feet gliding over the macadam, the rhythmic throbbing of his heart, his rotund frankness, his every meek and gentle detail. His growing joy and jubilation made his longing permeate all—from the sole of his feet out to infinite space, from the road he walked to the Firmament.

The earth in which the cameo was buried, under the Banner of the Scribes, had been dug up, one of the candy-pieces of the pyramid had been displaced a fraction of an inch, the ashes which made up the Knoll of the Imponderable still bore a fingerprint. Laceflies, frightened by S—'s presence, were immobile, as though encrusted to the glass panes of the roof. The minnows anxiously watched S—, their heads held out of the water.

"I knew from the first. From the moment the murderess killed for the first time, in the Cinema. As you know, I have been terribly distraught and overwrought by the crime . . . and intrigued. I went to the Bar not to ask questions but out of simple morbid curiosity. I wanted to know something more than what the newspapers reported. One of the waiters described the cameo in the brooch the murderess wore. It had attracted his attention, and he described it to me in wonderful detail. It was the first and last time the murderess wore it when she went out. But this brooch . . . I knew this brooch. I knew, probably even better than the waiter, what it looked like. My uncle, to be more precise, had received a drawing of it."

The pharaoh-ants had created a society in which the three compartments of a nest all coëxisted. I had constructed them in the image of the three spaces into which the human body was divided: the brain was the Palace of the Elixir of Immortality; the heart was the Red Battleground of Encounters; the lower belly, the loins, was the Palisaded Meadow of Work. Did S— erect impassable boundaries between those three territories? Would some innate border guard in him allow no passage from one to another? How deliciously his spirit was tending towards indolence! He wove strands of trifling weight into a fabric light as smoke.

"In the Castle you saw me as I am—a drunkard, a wreck. . . . What need have I to live? . . . to keep on in this world? . . . Who would ever miss me? . . . My uncle will not tolerate any longer the tragedy of having a nephew like me. A worthless, shiftless, ne'er-do-well . . . a wastrel and a flop. . . . Who will remember me if I cease to exist? What lips that I have kissed, what bodies that have possessed me, still bear any trace, show any sign, keep any memory, of me? What am I doing here? In this world?"

K— was crossing the plaza scant feet from the Mansion. I could see his figure approaching the Firmament as though the world had stopped and only he were moving. His body glowed with an inward light, while those bodies near him, around him, seemed to shed shadows.

How many autonomous subdivisions did each of the three spaces of S—'s body branch out into? The Hall of Governance of his head did not communicate with the Palace of Reality, nor did the Fortress of the Great Jester with the Garden of the Tremulous Pearl. Beneath his navel was situated the Pavilion of Passion, with its several independent wings. This edifice was separated by an impenetrable barrier from the Tower of Melancholy. In the joints of his hands and feet, in the tips of his fingers and toes, in the retinas of his eyes, there were sentinels awaiting messages from the outside which never came. The Immortal lived in the Garden of Events, while the Lord Male, who guided and channelled his destiny, held the Parapet of Spleen. Each of the edifices and its occupants—did they all issue their own laws? Prohibitions? Did they state recommendations? Did the administration of the three spaces invade everything secret and internal? Or did it but watch? Control? Not let pass? His fits and outbursts channelled into and then perished in the ocean of passion, but did the streams of affection still flow beneath?

"My body wears on me. If I had my way, I'd throw it onto a dungheap. I'd chuck it once and for all."

When one examined S— carefully one could make out the infinite features scattered through the three regions of his body. The Porch of Expectations lay between his eyebrows. In his brain, reigning separately in seventeen distinct Palaces, there were seventeen Princes all ignorant of one another's existence. The Adolescents of Adventure roller-skated through his temples, without any order or agreement. Those outside messages could only enter through the Centre of the Two Deaf Emperors located at the earlobes, where two typewriting monkeys took calls. When they wanted, they could ring the Bells of Fable so that the message would be received by the various Princes in their seventeen Palaces.

"I have carried out my own investigation of the murderess. My eyes would not at first see her, my ears hear her, or my mind understand her. I delved decisively, shrewdly, ingratiatingly—so cleverly, all in all, that one would have thought something outside myself, or some unknown internal force, were pushing me. . . . Do you know something? When I took you to see P— I hoped . . . you would sleep together. . . . I wanted to see him, through your eyes, naked, frail, helpless. I dreamt that you would tell me how he embraced you, how he touched you, penetrated you, kissed you. . . . But the two of you spent an entire week watching television every afternoon and evening. I wanted to discover how a man such as he, a genius, performed that secret, spontaneous act of physical love. . . . In reality, I sent you as a thief, without your knowing it yourself. Forgive me! . . . I wanted to know how P— painted his pictures. . . . For the very same reasons, I took you to the Castle . . . to D—'s party."

S—'s body—did there lodge in it venomous scorpions, perverse serpents, tell-tale beetles which tattled to the Head the Loins' mischief? Did it contain a Palace of Wonders which in its turn enclosed the inaccessible drug, the Elixir of Immortality? Had S— tried to force, rape, surreptitiously breach the wall which protected it? Did he not consider himself worthy of it? Did he imagine the Palace as a place with thousands of servants who led to the Tower of Tribute the privileged few who would receive from the King of Kings the gift of happiness? Did he paint immortality to himself as a brilliant, lovely liquid drop—which when touched clotted, its surface pitting and shrivelling into untold disgusting wrinkles? Why did S— so want his name to figure for century after century in the Register of Immortality? In the absurd silence of human enduring?

"I have failed—at everything. I would have liked to be a painter of real genius . . . though, had I achieved that, I'd have had to steal, rob, plagiarize, spread lies, sell my body or my soul, kill, prostitute myself. I sent you on a mission to P—'s Croft, and still I didn't know how to read the message. I couldn't decipher it. I couldn't figure it. It said simply: *'It's Fate's finger points.'* Unknowingly, you transmitted the word to me. I can do nothing to move that hand . . . to make it point at me."

I could sense every footstep K— took, mere yards away, as he neared the door to the Keep. They echoed sharply, fully, as though the street had been a vaulted nave.

Did S— pant so in order to breathe in the Essential, and yet only really respire, hold within his spirit, the Accidental? His breathing, as it penetrated his entire body, its rhythm, its pulse undulated through his veins from the tip of his nose to the last extreme of his twenty digits. Did that reflect the breathing of the newborn? The foetal respiration of him who cannot rise, be happy, immortal?, or of him who inverts the process of life without coming to die himself?

"Now I only want to die."

All S—'s energy—was it glued within the marrow of his bones? Could it only come out or be expressed in the form of caprices?

"Three years ago, the day after our return, P— wrote my uncle. He did not know he had only seven days left to live. In his letter he spoke almost entirely about you. You left such an impression on him! From the vantage point of his ninety-one years, he looked down enchanted on your fifteen. He explained to my uncle in that letter that when he thought of giving you a gift, he realised that you would never have appreciated one of his valuable paintings. And at any rate it was no ordinary present he wanted to give you. That is why it occurred to him at last to give you two objects which had meant something to him in his youth."

When K— came to the Keep, he found the door locked. I sensed his dismay, the quickened pulse of his breathing.

"You seem distracted. . . . You aren't listening to what I am trying to tell you. . . . Are you thinking of that ten-ton baby?"

Did S— attack K— the better to see his own nature? Did *pique* transform him into a visionary? Did he feel "called" by some external force and at the same time interrogated by it? Did that to-and-fro of question and response make him drunken? At last was revealed to him what neither his eyes nor his understanding could set before him. Deep within himself, did he fill his insomnia with tranced amazement?

"P— gave you the straight razor he had used to shave with when he was a young man. He gave you the object which best symbolized the awakening of his creativity. The cameo was his mother's—did you know?—the only thing he had left of hers after ninety-one years of life. He gave it to you not as a gift—it was a legacy. He willed it to you."

The Sisters and the Maimed One had now left for ever. They had boarded up the door to the Keep and run for the border in the car loaded down with boxes and bags. At the entrance to the Keep, sealed by them, K— wavered one instant. I felt him begin to hear my beating heart. I felt him be drawn by it to me.

S— persisted in his mistaken objectives:

"I knew from the first. From the very first murder. . . . The razor which was used to slit the throat in the Cinema was the one P— had used in his youth, the one he gave you. The murderess wore the cameo that had been P—'s mother's, the one he bequeathed to you, on her blouse."

S—'s voice chirped and squeaked through the Firmament. Was he trying to reach self-compassion? Self-aggression? From that lifeless hulk of gloom and anxiety?

"I will not allow the police to take you, or any judge to judge you. Leave me your bag. . . . You carry the razor in it . . . don't you?"

S— took the bag I carried to my Soirées. He took out P—'s razor. He studied it. Did S— think that any creature which inspires fear and horror might be venerated as a tutelary deity?

"You killed with this blade, the three of them. When all through these weeks I have told you, I who already knew everything, have told you bit by bit about the supposed stages of my investigation, you have behaved with utter and entire indifference. Why?"

K— walked all about the Mansion to go from the Keep to the Firmament. I could feel his footsteps on the other side of the thick walls of the Garden, and sense the centre of his self, his centre of equilibrium, inches below his navel, as though he were beside me.

S— agitatedly counted the seconds:

"Listen . . . I will turn my back to you . . . as your victims did. . . . My throat is bare. . . . Take the razor. . . . Do away with me!"

When K— arrived, outside, at the wall of the Firmament, I could hear his breathing through the barrier. His breath and mine marked the selfsame rhythm.

Were S—'s ears stopped by his illusions? His mind befuddled by the drug of suicide? Did death's slow coming torture him as though over live coals? Did he live through that slow torture as though through a thirst so parching that death became a mirage of oasis?

"Cut my throat! End it! Don't let me live a minute more. I suffer too much. One stroke . . . or . . . if not . . . I'll do it myself. . . . Here."

K— gave a violent shove. His shoulder crashed into the wall of the Firmament. The whole greenhouse shook to its very foundations. It was on the verge of collapsing.

S— absently cried:

"Give me the blade. . . . I can't wait a minute more."

K— threw himself a second time against the wall, putting

all his concentration, the whole art of *sumo* mastery, into the attempt. The wall collapsed into rubble. K— stepped slowly through the ruins, serene, through the dust and *débris,* from the other side of the Vigorous Mountains, over his shoulder the sack for our journey and in his hand the compass stone.

He said to me,

"Shall we go?"

I answered,

"Yes. Let's do go."